18^{00}

5755

A Kitchen Affair

Elizabethan Turkey. Recipe page 68.

A Kitchen Affair

Helen Fleming

Joint Publishers: South China Morning Post Ltd.,
Tong Chong Street, Quarry Bay, Hong Kong.

Four Corners Publishing Co. (Far East) Ltd.,
Suite 15A, 257 Gloucester Road, Hong Kong.

Photography by Benno Gross Associates
Design by Pat Printer Associates

Printed by Paramount Printing Company, Hong Kong.
19th Floor, North Point Industrial Building,
499 King's Road, Hong Kong.

Contents

Foreword

The majority of the recipes contained in this book are original, but I must confess I've borrowed certain others from my mother and my grandmother as well. Some are standard, such as sauces and pastries. There are several which are fairly difficult and time-consuming to prepare, but most of them have been designed with the average housewife in mind and are basically simple to cook.

Although a number of people have encouraged me to write this book and have been of great assistance, the most tremendous influence and inspiration came from my husband, Gordon. Without his help, blunt honesty and extreme patience I could not have succeeded.

Nor would I have become interested in the culinary arts if it had not been for my mother, who encouraged me when I was a child, taught me the basics and never made a fuss when she saw what a mess I'd made of the kitchen.

Some years ago, I found I wasn't satisfied with repeating other people's recipes; I wanted to experiment and create my own dishes. After moving to Hong Kong, I became intrigued by the cooking methods of the Far East, in particular its abundance of herbs and spices. You will see here that I've combined East and West in some of the recipes.

They have emerged from what can only be described as a lengthy period of trial and error, tossing out 'disasters,' improving upon and then perfecting the 'maybes,' and all the while filling up quite a few notebooks.

I also tested them on other people's palates and I must thank, in particular, our close friends Brigid and Neville Chesney, who served as guinea pigs and offered constructive criticism. Bless you both! And Major E.F.E. (Ted) Moorat and his wife Kate, who at their home in England taught me so much about the methods of hanging, cleaning, freezing and cooking game. My sincere thanks.

And to my many other friends, who, after tasting a few of my specialties such as Elizabethan Turkey and Curried Lobster Soup, convinced me I had quite enough material to write this book. Without their help and encouragement, it would have been an impossible task.

Finally, I hope you will find as much enjoyment in this book as I have had in writing it.

Helen Fleming

My special thanks are due to

Ferdinand Pieroth Weingut Weinkellerei GmbH
D6531 BURG LAYEN, Bei Bingen am Rhein
West Germany

Pieroth Hong Kong Ltd
17-33 Wang Lung Street
Tsuen Wan, N.T.
Hong Kong

Weights & Measures

Measurements in this edition are based on the metric system, although any ingredients used in quantities of less than 25 grams (25 g) or 25 millilitres (25 ml) have been given in teaspoon measures. Also, where it was considered more practical, certain ingredients are indicated by units, for example; 4 chicken breasts, 2 brown onions or 2 tomatoes. Unless otherwise stated, reference here is to medium size.

For those who think and work in Imperial measures there is a quick and simple conversion to keep in mind. That is taking 25 grams as being equal to 1 ounce and 25 millilitres as being equal to 1 fluid ounce. However, that is not completely accurate and while being satisfactory for small quantities, tends to become less practical as weights and measures become greater. The tables below will assist with more exact conversions but please take note of the added comment (*).

* For the professional chef, concerned with cost control and consistency, the quantities of various ingredients must be taken seriously. For the domestic cook, however, a too 'rigid' attitude toward weights and measures is seldom necessary and will tend to take away much of the pleasure from the joy of cooking. Many of the recipes in this book involve a plentiful use of spices and bear in mind that individual palates must always be taken into consideration when preparing these dishes.

Weights and measures

Ounces/ fluid ounces	Approx. gramme and millilitre to nearest whole figure	Recommended conversion to nearest unit of 25
1	28	25
2	57	50
3	85	75
4	113	100
5	142	150
6	170	175
7	198	200
8	226	225
9	255	250
10	283	275
11	311	300
r2	340	350
13	368	375
14	396	400
15	428	425
16 (1 lb)	456	450
17	484	475
18	512	500
19	541	550
20	569	575
27	767	750
35 (2lb 3oz)	1,000 (1 kilogram)	1,000

Liquid Equivalents

Imperial	Metric (ml)	American measures (cup)
1 (fl oz)	25 (ml)	
	50	$\frac{1}{4}$ (cup)
	125	$\frac{1}{2}$
$\frac{1}{4}$ (pint)	150	
	200	$\frac{3}{4}$
	250	1
$\frac{1}{2}$	300	$1\frac{1}{4}$
	375	$1\frac{1}{2}$
	(450)	(American pint)
	500	2
1	550	
	750	3
$2\frac{3}{4}$	1,000 (1 litre)	4
3	1,150	

Volume Measurements

Ingredient	Metric	Imperial	American
Flour	220 g	7 oz	2 cups
Sugar, granulated	220 g	7 oz	1 cup
Rice	220 g	7 oz	1 cup
Peanuts, shelled	350 g	12 oz	$1\frac{1}{2}$ cups
Cornstarch	25 g	1 oz	1 level tablespoon
Sugar, castor	25 g	1 oz	1 level tablespoon

Soups & Stocks

Most soups are made from basic stocks which no well-equipped kitchen should be without. The average housewife does not always have the time or energy to make her own stock from scratch, therefore a good supply of commercial stock cubes or powder should be kept on hand.

However, for that extra special dinner party or other such occasion, the added flavour of good, rich home-made stock in purées, soups, gravies, sauces etc., will enhance any dish.

Taking some time and a little imagination, the following recipes can be adapted for any use. Left-over meat from roasts, giblets, vegetables, bones, bacon rinds and many other footstuffs can be used as well as fresh ingredients.

Most stocks freeze very well, so it is best to make them in large quantities. Reserve sufficient for immediate use then store the remainder in different sized containers (for thrift and convenience) and place in the freezer until ready for use.

Use of cooked ingredients from stocks:

Meats:	Use in hash, stews, ragouts, estouffades, purées, and thick soups.
Vegetables:	In most cases, discard unless stated otherwise.
Stock:	Soups, purées, sauces, gravies, ragouts, estouffades, casseroles and stews.
Fat:	If stock is to be kept refrigerated for several days prior to use, leave the fat intact as it acts as a sealing agent. When ready for use, remove fat carefully and use for roasting dark meats, gravies, or making a roux. In most cases, fat can be frozen for short periods of time.

Types of Stocks:

There are many types and variations, but the recipes on the following pages are the main basic stocks such as chicken, brown (light and dark), fish, game, veal and vegetable.

To 'clarify' stock, refer to 'Glossary'.

BROWN STOCK — LIGHT

**1 kilo beef, veal or poultry bones
and meat**
500 g ham bone or knuckle
3 rashers streaky bacon
3 carrots
3 large onions
50 g dripping
1 bay leaf
1 bouquet garni
6 whole black peppercorns
salt to taste
water to cover

Make slices in the meat, going through to the bone but without completely removing meat. Peel and slice vegetables. If meats and vegetables are fresh, i.e. not previously cooked, fry in dripping until sealed but not brown. Place in a large saucepan together with the other ingredients and slowly bring the the boil, removing any scum as it comes to the top. Reduce heat and simmer with the lid on for at least 8 hours. As the cooking time is very slow, check water level at regular intervals and 'top up' when necessary. Skim off all the fat and strain through a fine sieve. Leave to settle until cooled and, if required straight away, scrape solidified fat from the top. If stock is not to be used immediately, leave the fat intact to 'seal' the stock until ready for use.

BROWN STOCK — DARK

**Ingredients as for light
stock (above) plus:**
25 g plain flour
225 ml red wine

Trim the fat from meat and cut to loosen slightly from the bones. Peel and slice vegetables. Melt dripping in a heavy-based pan and fry meat and vegetables separately until well browned on all sides. (This applies whether ingredients have been previously cooked or not). Reserve meat and vegetables. Sprinkle the flour into the pan and stir for 5 minutes, remove from heat and gradually add the red wine, stirring continuously until the mixture has thickened and is thoroughly blended. Transfer ingredients to a 4-kilo saucepan, add 200 ml of cold water and stir until smooth. Return saucepan to heat and slowly bring back to the boil. Add meat and vegetables, reduce heat to simmer and add remaining ingredients. Continue in the same manner as for light stock.

FISH STOCK

**1½ kilos fish heads, bones, tails,
trimmings, plus any white
flesh**
575 ml water
220 ml dry white wine
1 stalk of celery, sliced
1 carrot, sliced
1 large onion, diced
1 pinch basil
1 pinch thyme
1 bay leaf
25 ml lemon juice
salt and white pepper to taste

Place fish heads, bones, tails, trimmings and flesh into a saucepan with water and dry white wine. Lightly sauté the celery, carrot and onion separately in butter until golden brown. Add to fish and bring slowly to the boil. When water is boiling rapidly, add remaining ingredients and cook for 20 minutes. Reduce heat and simmer for 2 hours, checking water level at regular intervals. Remove from heat, strain through a fine sieve or muslin cloth and when cool, refrigerate until ready for use. Use for basis of thick fish soup, court-bouillon or bouillabaisse.

CHICKEN STOCK

1¼ kilos chicken, turkey or duck
    carcass, bones, giblets (except
    liver) plus any left-over meat
2 brown onions
1 carrot
1 stalk of celery
1 cooking apple
3 cloves
6 whole black peppercorns
1 pinch sage
1 pinch thyme
salt to taste
225 ml dry white wine

Place all the meat, bones, giblets and carcass into a large saucepan. Peel and quarter the onions, slice carrot and celery and add to pan together with the peeled whole apple stuck with cloves, and remaining ingredients. Add sufficient water to completely cover and slowly bring to the boil. Allow to boil gently for 30 minutes, top up water level, remove scum, cover then reduce heat to simmer and cook for a further 2 hours. Remove from heat and allow to cool. Strain through a colander and place stock in refrigerator until the fat solidifies. Remove fat if for immediate use otherwise leave intact.

VEAL STOCK

1½ kilos veal knuckle, shoulder
    or other cuts
450 g ham meat and bone
1 carrot, sliced
1 stalk celery, sliced
2 onions, quartered
1 potato, diced
1 pinch sage
1 pinch thyme
6 whole black peppercorns
salt to taste

Cut meat away slightly from bones. Place meat and prepared vegetables in a large saucepan, cover with water and slowly bring to the boil. Add remaining ingredients and boil for 20 minutes, reduce to simmer and cook for a further 2 hours, topping up water level if necessary and removing scum as it comes to the top. Remove from heat, strain through a colander and set aside to cool. Remove fat and refrigerate or freeze until ready for use.

VEGETABLE STOCK

2 carrots
2 large onions
2 leeks
1 stalk celery
1 parsnip
100 g green beans
100 g green peas
100 g broccoli
50 g butter
25 g chopped parsley
1 pinch thyme
1 bay leaf
1 bouquet garni
salt to taste
freshly ground black pepper

Prepare the vegetables and chop roughly. Melt the butter in a frying pan and add carrots, onions, leeks and celery and 'stir-fry' for 3 to 4 minutes or until vegetables just begin to darken in colour. Remove from frying pan, drain and place in a large saucepan together with remaining ingredients. Add 1½ litres of cold water and bring to the boil. Reduce heat, cover and simmer for 1½ hours.
Strain and use as required.
NOTE: Depending on availability or preference, the same basic recipe may be used substituting other vegetables such as shallots, swedes, brussels sprouts, cabbage and spinach.

GAME STOCK

3 litres water
900 g trimmings from hare
    (or rabbit)
675 g venison (shoulder, knuckle
    or breast)
1 pheasant
1 partridge
1 pigeon or quail
1 carrot
1 onion
1 clove
1 bouquet garni
1 sprig fresh rosemary
8 juniper berries
225 g rice
50 g dripping
25 g butter
575 ml red wine
salt and pepper to taste

Prepare meat by trussing pheasant, partridge and pigeon (or quail), tie venison in place by rolling meat and securing with string. Place in a roasting dish with dripping and hare trimmings. Roast in a moderate oven for 30 minutes. Prepare vegetables, slice and brown in a pan with butter. Remove meat from oven and cut into small pieces, add to pan with vegetables and cook for 10 minutes, turning meat so that all sides are nicely browned. Place meat, vegetables and pan drippings into a large saucepan, cover with water and slowly bring to the boil, reduce heat and simmer for 4 hours, skimming occasionally. Add red wine and remaining ingredients and simmer for a further 2 hours. Strain through a colander and set aside to cool. Place in refrigerator overnight or until fat solidifies then carefully scrape all fat from the surface. This stock can be frozen until ready for use. The fat can be used for roasting duck, goose, turkey and game.

RICH STOCK

Take any left-over meat and
    vegetables from roasts and
    make up the full quantities
    with fresh ingredients as
    follows:
900 g meat (beef, poultry,
    veal, ham)
1 turnip
2 large onions
2 potatoes
1 carrot
1 stalk celery, including
    leaf end
100 g broccoli
50 g brussels sprouts
2 leeks
3 tomatoes
50 g chopped parsley
1 pinch basil
1 pinch thyme
1 pinch marjoram
8 whole black peppercorns
1 bay leaf
salt to taste

Prepare all vegetables, chop roughly and place in a saucepan with meat, cover with water and bring to the boil. Reduce heat and simmer for 3 hours. Add remaining ingredients and continue to cook for a further 1½ hours. Strain through a fine sieve then return stock to a clean saucepan and simmer for another 1 hour. Re-strain and allow to cool. When quite cold, remove fat from the top. (There will be very little fat if fresh vegetables and previously cooked meats are used). This stock is excellent for the basis of rich gravy or brown casseroles and stews.

Chilled Pumpkin Soup/Potato and Leek Soup

CHILLED PUMPKIN SOUP

Half a pumpkin (preferably butternut)
2 large potatoes
1 onion
1½ litres vegetable stock
1 teaspoon cumin seed
2 cloves garlic
50 g butter
1 leek
1 pinch turmeric
salt and pepper to taste
1 teaspoon paprika

serves 6

Peel pumpkin, potatoes and onion and dice finely. Place in a saucepan together with vegetable stock and slowly bring to the boil, reduce heat and simmer for 15 minutes. Using a mortar and pestle, pound the cumin seed and garlic cloves and add to stock. Simmer for a further 5 minutes. Melt the butter in a frying pan and add the chopped leek. Fry until soft but not brown and add to stock. Continue cooking for a further 10 minutes then remove from heat and stir in the turmeric. Using a wooden spoon and a very fine sieve, strain the stock mixture into a bowl, forcing the vegetables through the sieve to form a purée. Stir thoroughly and when well blended add salt and pepper to taste. Transfer to a soup tureen, sprinkle paprika on top and place in refrigerator until ready for use. Serve very cold.

POTATO AND LEEK SOUP

6 medium potatoes
3 large leeks
1 large brown onion
800 ml water or vegetable stock
8 spring onions
1 clove garlic
450 ml milk
225 ml cream
salt and pepper to taste

serves 6

Peel and roughly chop the potatoes and leeks, peel and grate onion and place in a saucepan with water or stock, bring to the boil, reduce heat to simmer and cook for 35 minutes or until vegetables are quite soft. Chop 5 of the spring onions and add to soup. Cook for a further 5 minutes. Remove from heat, strain, then force the vegetables through a coarse strainer or place in an electric blender and blend until puréed. Whisk the stock and purée together until well blended then gradually stir in the milk and cream. Add salt and pepper to taste then place soup in a container, cover and refrigerate for at least 4 hours. Just prior to serving, chop the remaining spring onions and sprinkle on top of soup. Serve very cold.

CHILLED WATERCRESS SOUP

300 g watercress
1 onion
1 clove garlic
1 litre chicken stock
225 ml milk
50 ml lemon juice
100 ml cream
salt and pepper to taste

serves 4

Remove stalks from watercress, rinse leaves and smaller tender stalks in clean water then pat dry with a kitchen towel. Place in blender with grated onion, crushed clove of garlic and half the chicken stock. Blend for 3 minutes then pour into a large bowl. With a wire whisk, beat in the remaining ingredients, except cream. Just prior to serving stir in the cream and season to taste with salt and pepper. Garnish with parsley sprigs. This soup must be served ice cold.

NOTE: To maintain the pungent flavour of this soup, the watercress is not cooked.

CHILLED GREEN VEGETABLE SOUP

1 packet frozen broccoli
1 packet frozen spinach
1 packet frozen green beans
850 ml vegetable stock
850 ml milk
4 spring onions
2 teaspoons garlic salt
2 teaspoons cumin seed
1 teaspoon cayenne pepper
salt and white pepper to taste

serves 6

Place all frozen vegetables in a saucepan, add stock and slowly bring to the boil. Reduce heat and when vegetables are defrosted, remove from heat and allow to cool. (If you do not have any stock on hand, defrost the vegetables in water, reserve liquid and use as stock.) Place vegetables, milk, chopped spring onions, garlic salt, cumin seed and cayenne pepper in a blender. When puréed, place in a bowl and stir in enough stock to reach desired consistency. Add salt and white pepper to taste, cover and refrigerate until ready for use.

NOTE: This is a very quick and easy dish to make. It is very tasty and is ideal for last minute guests for dinner.

GARLIC SOUP

20 cloves garlic
2 litres water
1 pinch thyme
1 pinch sage
6 eggs
salt
pepper
24 slices french bread

serves 6

Peel and crush the garlic cloves and place in a saucepan together with the water and herbs. Bring to the boil and boil rapidly for 30 minutes. Season to taste with salt and black pepper. Prior to serving, break the eggs into individual bowls, pour the hot soup over and serve immediately with slices of french bread which is dipped into the soup when eating.

NOTE: This soup must be served piping hot in order to poach the eggs slightly before serving.

CURRIED LOBSTER SOUP

1 lobster tail
1 litre fish stock
200 g butter
1 medium onion, grated
2 teaspoons basil
50 g curry powder
75 g tomato paste
75 ml olive oil
500 ml milk
100 g flour
75 g chopped chives
100 ml brandy
100 ml cream
salt and pepper to taste

serves 6

Place fish stock in a large saucepan and bring to the boil, reduce heat and simmer. Remove meat from lobster tail and chop finely, add to stock and cook for 10 minutes. Melt half the butter in a frying pan and add the grated onion and basil. Cook until onion is soft but not browned. Using a little of the olive oil, blend curry powder and tomato paste until smooth, then slowly add the remaining oil. Add curry mixture to onions in the frying pan and cook, stirring all the time, until a red, oily film appears on top of the mixture. Add to lobster stock. Make a roux by melting the remaining butter, blend in flour and cook over a low heat for 1 minute. Remove from heat and gradually stir in the milk. When smooth, return to heat and stir until thickened. Pour this sauce into the lobster stock and allow to simmer for a further 10 minutes without boiling. Add chopped chives to the soup and stir in the brandy and cream. Remove from heat and add salt and pepper to taste. Serve immediately.

ICED SPINACH SOUP

225 g fresh spinach leaves
1 potato
1 onion
450 ml chicken stock
25g mustard seeds
1 teaspoon cumin seeds
3 cloves garlic
175 ml olive oil
50 ml wine vinegar
225 ml milk
salt
freshly ground black pepper

GARNISH
chopped parsley
1 spring onion, sliced
25 g cucumber, diced
ice cubes

serves 6

Chop stalks from spinach leaves and cut into chunks. Peel and dice potato and onion. Place chicken stock in a saucepan, add potato and onion and slowly bring to the boil. Add chopped spinach stalks and allow to cook for 8 minutes. Remove from heat and allow to cool slightly. Wash the spinach leaves and pat dry. Chop roughly and add to soup, place the lid on top and allow to cool completely. Meanwhile, place the mustard seeds, cumin seeds, crushed garlic, oil and vinegar in a blender and mix for 1 minute or until the mixture is smooth. Pour the cold stock into blender and blend until the spinach leaves are properly puréed. Place in a bowl or tureen in the refrigerator until quite cold. Just before serving, stir in milk, salt and pepper to taste. Garnish with parsley, spring onion, cucumber and ice cubes.

NOTE: For a richer soup, use half milk and half cream.
For a novel idea, all garnish ingredients can be frozen into ice blocks and placed whole in the soup just before serving. It makes a very attractive dish.

Curried Lobster Soup/Iced Spinach Soup

CREAMY PRAWN SOUP

1 kilo prawns
1½ litres fish stock
1 pinch thyme
1 bay leaf
1 litre milk
50 g flour
50 g butter
50 ml lemon juice
2 teaspoons paprika

serves 6

Put fish stock, thyme and bay leaf in a saucepan and bring to the boil. Place live or frozen prawns in the boiling stock and cook for 4 minutes. Reduce heat and simmer for a further 4 minutes. Remove prawns and set aside to cool slightly. Increase the heat and reduce stock by half, strain and reserve. Shell and clean the prawns and reserve. Use a little of the cold milk and blend the flour until smooth. Place remaining milk in a saucepan with the reserved stock and heat through gently without boiling. Add butter and when melted, slowly stir in the flour and lemon juice. Season to taste with salt and pepper, then add the prawns to soup and heat through. Pour into a tureen and sprinkle with paprika.

CORN AND CRABMEAT SOUP

500 g whole corn kernels
1¼ litres chicken stock
50 g butter
1 onion
25 mm piece fresh ginger root
225 g crabmeat
1 egg
salt and pepper
2 spring onions

serves 4

Use fresh, tinned or frozen kernels and place in a saucepan with the chicken stock. Slowly bring to the boil, reduce heat and simmer for 15 minutes. Heat the butter in a frying pan and gently fry the whole peeled onion for a few minutes without browning. Add to soup together with the whole piece of ginger root and simmer for 30 minutes. Add the crabmeat and cook for a further 15 minutes. Remove and discard the onion and ginger root. Beat the egg and slowly pour into the soup in a thin stream so it gives a 'curdled' appearance. Add salt and pepper to taste. Serve immediately garnished with chopped spring onions.

CHEESE SOUP

1½ litres water
1 onion
1 carrot
1 turnip
1 stalk celery
1 bay leaf
50 g cornflour
200 ml milk
2 eggs
50 ml cream
225 g grated gruyère cheese
25 g parsley
salt and pepper to taste

serves 6

Place water in a large saucepan. Peel the onion, carrot and turnip and slice roughly. Chop the celery and place in saucepan together with the other vegetables and bay leaf. Bring to the boil, reduce heat and simmer for 1½ hours. Strain the stock through a colander and discard vegetables. Put stock into a clean saucepan. Blend the cornflour with a little cold water and stir into stock. When slightly thickened, add the milk and cook, without boiling, for 15 minutes. Beat the egg yolks and whisk into soup. Add salt and pepper to taste then gradually add the cream. Place grated cheese in a warm soup tureen and pour the hot soup over, stirring until blended. Sprinkle the top with chopped parsley and serve immediately with slices of french bread.

ESCARGOT À LA CRÈME

24 escargots
50 g butter
50 ml olive oil
75 g fresh mushrooms
2 cloves garlic, crushed
2 onions
50 ml brandy
450 ml dry white wine
25 g sugar
75 g parsley, chopped
50 g chives, chopped
2 pinches thyme
1 pinch marjoram
50 ml lemon juice
225 ml cream
salt and pepper to taste

serves 4

Place half the butter in a frying pan and heat through slowly, add half the oil and fry the sliced mushrooms until soft, remove from pan and reserve. Fry the crushed garlic and chopped onions until soft but not browned, remove and reserve with the mushrooms. Place the escargots in the pan and cook for 5 minutes, pour brandy over and when boiling, set alight and flame the escargots. Place the white wine in a saucepan with sugar, remaining butter and oil, add herbs and heat through gently. Simmer for 10 minutes then add the lemon juice. Stir in the mushrooms, garlic, onion and escargots and simmer for a further 10 minutes. Remove from heat and gradually stir in the cream. Add salt and pepper to taste, return to heat (do not allow to boil) and keep warm until ready for serving. Garnish with a few sprigs of fresh tarragon.

FISH SOUP

450 g assorted fish (pomfret, yellow thread, mullet, sole, whiting, etc.)
3 onions
2 cloves garlic
75 ml olive oil
1 teaspoon rosemary
1 teaspoon sage
½ teaspoon thyme
25 g parsley
1 bay leaf
1 teaspoon dried fennel
6 whole black peppercorns
75 g tomato purée
2 litres fish stock
1 lemon
salt and pepper to taste

serves 4

Prepare, wash and wipe fish — leave whole. Heat the olive oil in a frying pan and gently fry the chopped onions and crushed garlic cloves. When a golden colour, add rosemary, sage, thyme, parsley, bay leaf, fennel, peppercorns and tomato purée. Cook for 2 minutes stirring continuously to prevent sticking. Slowly add 2 litres of stock, add the fish, bring to the boil then reduce heat and simmer. Squeeze juice from lemon and add both juice and rind to the stock. Bring back to the boil and boil for 5 minutes. Reduce heat and simmer with lid on for 30 minutes. Remove bay leaf and lemon rind and discard. Remove fish and place on a chopping board. Using a fork, flake the meat away from the bones and discard the head, tail, trimmings and bones. Add flesh to soup, and pour into an electric blender. Blend at high speed for 1 minute and when puréed return soup to pan and keep hot. Season to taste with salt and pepper prior to serving.

SPICY TOMATO SOUP

850 g ripe tomatoes
50 g butter
850 ml cold water
1 teaspoon sugar
2 small onions
50 g parsley
50 g mixed herbs
1 bouquet garni
1 pinch bicarbonate of soda
25 g flour
225 ml milk
salt
black pepper

serves 4

Place whole tomatoes, half the butter, water, sugar, peeled and chopped onions, parsley, mixed herbs and bouquet garni in a saucepan and slowly bring to the boil. Reduce heat and simmer with the lid on for approximately 1½ hours or until the tomatoes and onions are quite soft. Add a pinch of bicarbonate of soda then push the mixture through a mouli or a coarse strainer. Make a béchamel sauce by melting the remaining butter in a frying pan, stir in the sifted flour and cook over a low heat for 1 minute. Remove from heat and gradually add the milk, stirring until smooth. Return to the heat and cook for 2 minutes or until mixture thickens enough to coat the back of a wooden spoon. Add to tomato soup, re-heat but do not boil. Season to taste with salt and freshly ground black pepper.

CHILLED AVOCADO SOUP

3 medium avocados
1 large onion
2 medium garlic cloves
850 ml milk
175 ml cream
50 ml lemon juice
salt and pepper to taste

serves 6

Cut avocados in half and remove stones. Peel away skin and slice roughly, reserving 3 or 4 whole slices for garnishing. Place the avocado in a blender with chopped onion, crushed garlic, milk and cream. Blend for 3 minutes then add lemon juice, salt and pepper to taste. If a thinner or less rich soup is required, extra milk or chicken stock may be used in place of cream. Garnish the soup with slices of avocado, parsley and lemon twists. Refrigerate until very cold.

Chilled Avocado Soup

SPLIT PEA AND HAM SOUP

1 large ham bone
1 veal knuckle
400 g split peas
1 ½ litres water
1 carrot
2 onions
¼ teaspoon bicarbonate of soda
25 g chopped parsley
salt
white pepper

serves 6

Wash the peas, cover with cold water and allow to stand for at least 3 hours. Drain and replace in a saucepan with 1 ½ litres of water, ham and veal bones. Slowly bring to the boil, reduce heat and cook uncovered for 1 hour. Scrape and slice the carrot, peel and quarter the onions and add to soup stock. Continue to cook for a further 2 hours, topping up water level if necessary. Remove the bones, reserving meat from the ham bone and discarding the veal bone. Put stock and vegetables through a coarse strainer or mouli, add bicarbonate of soda, parsley and seasonings. Remove meat from ham bone and chop finely. Add to soup. Re-heat and serve.

PORTUGUESE GREEN VEGETABLE SOUP

850 g potatoes
1 ¼ litres chicken or vegetable stock
1 whole chorizo sausage
150 g whole leaf spinach
100 ml vinegar
200 ml olive oil
salt
pepper
oil and vinegar to taste

serves 4

Peel potatoes and cut into cubes. Place stock in a saucepan and add potatoes, whole sausage and a little vinegar. When potatoes are quite cooked, remove sausage, slice and reserve. Force the potato and stock through a fine sieve with a wooden spoon, then whip it until the purée is smooth. Cut the spinach 'julienne' style and add to the purée. Bring back to the boil and add reserved sausage. Reduce heat and simmer for 5 minutes, then remove from heat and whip the remaining oil and vinegar into the soup. Place in a tureen and serve very hot. Serve with additional oil and vinegar according to taste and adjust seasoning with salt and white pepper.

CREAM OF ASPARAGUS SOUP

450 g fresh or tinned asparagus
1 ½ litres vegetable stock
2 onions
2 potatoes
1 stalk celery
1 leek
1 bouquet garni
450 ml cream
2 egg yolks
salt
white pepper

serves 4

Wash asparagus and pat dry. Scrape stalks and trim off ends, leaving 25 mm of white flesh. Place in a saucepan with vegetable stock and bring to the boil. Peel and dice the onions, potatoes, wash celery and leek and cut into 4 pieces. Add to stock with bouquet garni, reduce heat and simmer for 1 hour. Remove celery, leek and bouquet garni from stock and discard. Place remaining vegetables and stock in a blender and blend until puréed. Return liquid to saucepan and heat through gently. Mix 50 ml of cream with the egg yolks and a little hot stock. When well blended pour into soup, stirring to prevent lumps. Do not allow to boil. Season to taste with salt and white pepper. Divide the remaining cream equally and place in 4 individual bowls. Pour the asparagus soup over the cream and serve immediately.

HOTCH POTCH

1 ½ litres rich stock
1 kilo meat (mutton, veal, ham)
75 g butter
2 onions, sliced roughly
1 carrot, sliced
1 leek, sliced
1 stalk celery, sliced
1 turnip, diced
2 Jerusalem artichokes, sliced
3 tomatoes
1 bay leaf
100 g lettuce
100 g cabbage
6 whole black peppercorns
50 g flour
50 ml milk
salt to taste

serves 6 to 8

Place stock in a large saucepan and add the trimmed meat. Bring to the boil, reduce heat and simmer for 1 ½ hours removing scum as it comes to the top and topping up water level at regular intervals. Heat a little of the butter and gently sauté the onions until soft. Drain on kitchen paper and add to stock. Use remaining butter and sauté the carrot, leek, celery, turnip and artichokes. When vegetables are nicely browned, drain and add to stock. Pour boiling water over the tomatoes to crack skins. Remove skins and chop flesh roughly. Add tomatoes to stock together with bay leaf and cook for a further 1 hour. Strain stock, reserving meat and vegetables. Pour stock into a clean saucepan and add the lettuce, cabbage and crushed black peppercorns. Allow stock to boil for 15 minutes then reduce heat and cook for 10 minutes. Strain and discard lettuce and cabbage. Return stock to saucepan again and add salt and pepper to taste. Blend the flour with a little milk and when smooth, stir in the remaining milk. Beat this mixture into the stock with a wire whisk and continue to whisk until quite smooth. Chop the reserved meat finely and add to stock together with vegetables (optional), adjust seasoning and heat through without boiling. Keep soup warm until ready for serving. This is a hearty soup and is ideal for cold winter months.

Chicken Consommé/Red Lentil Soup

CHICKEN CONSOMME

750 g chicken bones and left-over flesh

2 medium onions, quartered

1 carrot, sliced

8-10 whole black peppercorns

2 stalks celery, roughly chopped

2 large potatoes, diced

1 teaspoon basil

1 teaspoon thyme

2 teaspoons rock salt

2 egg whites and shells

cold water to cover

serves 4

Place all above ingredients except egg whites and shells into a large saucepan. Bring slowly to the boil then reduce heat and simmer with the lid on for at least 3 hours. Cool and remove fat from top (this may necessitate refrigerating for several hours to solidify the fat). Strain through a colander lined with a double layer of muslin. Return stock to clean pan and add egg whites and their shells. Whisk continuously whilst bringing to the boil and continue whisking for 10 minutes. Strain through a fine sieve lined with double muslin and season to taste with salt and pepper. If a clearer consommé is required, return stock to pan and add one egg white and one shell, whisking as before and continue the recipe from there. This consommé is suitable for freezing but if it is being kept in the refrigerator for any length of time, reboil for 5 minutes every 3 days in summer and every 5 days in winter.

RED LENTIL SOUP

225 g haricot beans

2 litres water

25 g butter

1 pinch bicarbonate of soda

225 g tomatoes

2 onions

1 parsnip

1 stalk celery

1 small beetroot

salt and pepper

serves 6

Soak the beans in cold water overnight. Strain the beans and rinse in fresh water. Place in a saucepan with 2 litres of fresh water, butter, and a pinch of bicarbonate of soda. Bring to the boil then reduce heat slightly and place lid on. Peel and chop tomatoes, onions and parsnip, chop celery and add to soup. Peel the raw beetroot and slice thinly, add to soup. Allow soup to come back to the boil, boil rapidly for 15 minutes then reduce heat, re-cover and simmer for 3 hours, topping up water level if necessary. Strain through a colander, remove haricot beans and force through a sieve. Discard remaining vegetables. Season with salt and pepper, re-heat and keep warm until ready for serving.

BEETROOT SOUP

1 kilo fresh beetroot
450 ml water
450 ml vegetable stock
2 onions
1 potato
1 turnip
2 eggs
25 ml lemon juice
250 ml sour cream
salt and pepper to taste

serves 6

Wash the beetroot thoroughly and place in a saucepan with water and a little salt. Bring to the boil and cook for 30 minutes. Strain off liquid and reserve. Peel and finely dice the beetroot, peel and dice the onions, potato and turnip. Put all the vegetables in a large saucepan with reserved liquid and vegetable stock, bring to the boil, reduce heat to simmer and cook for 1½ hours. Remove from heat and mash the vegetables with a potato masher. Using a little of the sour cream and hot liquid, mix the egg yolks and add to the soup. Heat through gently without boiling and stir until soup thickens. Add salt and pepper to taste. Just prior to serving pour the soup into a tureen or individual bowls and lightly stir in the remaining sour cream. Serve immediately.

EASTERN MINESTRONE

2 carrots
2 potatoes
2 onions
2 leeks
1 parsnip
2 stalks celery
2 cloves garlic
100 ml olive oil
4 tomatoes
2 litres vegetable stock
175 g peas
1 teaspoon basil
1 teaspoon chervil
1 teaspoon sweet marjoram
1 teaspoon ginger powder
175 g red lentils, soaked
　　overnight
100 g green lima beans
50 g large vermicelli
100 ml dry sherry
salt and pepper to taste
5 spring onions
100 g parmesan cheese

serves 6-8

Peel and finely dice the carrots, potatoes and onions. Wash and finely slice the leeks, parsnip and celery, peel and crush garlic. Heat the oil in a heavy-based frying pan and gently sauté the vegetables until soft. Pour some boiling water over the tomatoes to crack skins, drain and set aside to cool slightly, then remove skins and discard. Chop the tomatoes finely and add to sautéed vegetables. Bring the stock to the boil, reduce heat and add sautéed vegetables, peas, basil, chervil, sweet marjoram and ginger powder and simmer gently for 30 minutes. Add the red lentils, lima beans and vermicelli and cook for a further 30 minutes. Season to taste with salt and pepper. Just prior to serving, pour in the dry sherry and sprinkle the top with chopped spring onions. Serve with freshly grated parmesan cheese.

GAME CONSOMMÉ

1 pheasant
1 partridge
1 mallard or other wild duck
500 g rabbit or hare
4 rashers back bacon
50 g butter or lard
2¼ litres game or chicken stock
2 onions
2 carrots
2 stalks celery
8 juniper berries
3 cloves
1 teaspoon marjoram
1 teaspoon basil
1 teaspoon mace
25 ml lemon juice
300 ml port dregs
salt and pepper
2 egg whites and shells

serves 6

Remove meat from the game and wipe with a dry cloth. Chop into large chunks. Place the butter in a heavy-based frying pan and when melted fry the game pieces over high heat until nicely browned on all sides and meat is sealed. Place meat in a large saucepan. Chop the bacon roughly and fry in the same pan. Add to saucepan together with bones, giblets (except liver) and stock and bring to the boil. Peel and chop the onions into quarters. Scrape and slice the carrots and celery and place in stock. Boil for 15 minutes then reduce heat to simmer. Using a mortar and pestle, crush the juniper berries, cloves, marjoram, basil and mace until finely ground, mix with the lemon juice and add to stock. Simmer gently with the lid on for 5 hours, removing scum as it comes to the top and topping up water level if necessary. Add the port dregs and simmer for a further 1 hour. Remove from heat and strain off liquid, discarding bones, giblets and vegetables. Reserve a little of the meat. Place the strained stock into a clean saucepan and add the whites and shells of eggs. Bring to the boil whisking all the time. Boil rapidly for 10 minutes then remove from heat and strain through a fine sieve lined with a double layer of muslin. Add salt and pepper to taste. Before serving, finely chop some of the meat, place in a soup tureen and pour the consommé over. Garnish with sprigs of parsley and lemon twists.

OXTAIL SOUP

1¼ kilos oxtail
225 g red lentils
3 carrots
2 leeks
3 onions
2¼ litres stock or water
1 turnip
1 stalk celery
1 potato
50 g butter
50 g flour
50 ml sherry

serves 6

Wipe oxtail and trim off surplus fat. Soak the lentils in cold water overnight if possible or for at least 4 hours. Place oxtail, lentils, peeled and sliced carrots, leeks and onions in a saucepan with the stock or water and slowly bring to the boil. Boil for 10 minutes then reduce heat, cover and simmer for 5 hours. Strain liquid and reserve. Remove meat from bones and reserve. Discard vegetables and bones. Place the stock in a pan and add peeled and sliced turnip, celery and potato. Simmer for a further 2 hours with lid off. Re-strain and discard vegetables. Melt the butter in a frying pan and stir in the sifted flour. Cook over a moderately high heat for 3 minutes or until roux turns brown. Remove from heat and slowly stir in some of the oxtail soup and continue stirring and adding soup until mixture is smooth. Pour into remaining soup, re-heat stirring all the time to prevent lumps and keep warm until ready for use. Season to taste and add dry sherry and reserved meat just before serving.

Salads & Entrées

As these dishes are designed as a prelude to the main course, the more simple the dish, the more it will be appreciated.

If a heavy or filling entrée is being served, then it should be served in small quantities so as not to ruin the appetite for better things to come.

Some Do's and Don'ts

Do: Select a recipe which is complementary to the main course.

Don't: Serve the same type of food for both courses i.e. fish entrée, fish main course.

Do: Vary the flesh colours i.e. if fish is served first it should be followed by a dark meat and vice versa.

Don't: Use brown or white sauces for both dishes.

Do: Use attractive garnishes — it makes the helpings look more generous and interesting.

Don't: Prepare a hot or spicy entrée if it is being followed by a milder tasting main course as the flavour of the entrée will overpower the food to be served next. If the entrée is quite pungent then a sorbet should be served between courses to cleanse the palate.

The above points will be appreciated by your guests when they see how cleverly you've prepared the menu. Instead of not being able to eat all of the main course or dessert, your guests should be fully repleted after finishing and enjoying all courses — remember — they can always come back for second helpings, which is the best compliment any cook can receive. "The proof of the pudding is in the eating."

PRAWN AND ONION SALAD

1 kilo fresh prawns
275 ml lemon juice
275 ml olive oil
1 teaspoon tarragon
salt and black pepper
1 onion
25 g parsley

serves 6

If prawns are still alive, place them in a large saucepan of rapidly boiling water to which 150 ml of dry white wine has been added. Boil for 4 minutes then reduce heat slightly and cook for a further 4 to 5 minutes, depending on the size of the prawns. Drain and set aside to cool down then peel away shells, remove any dirty pieces then rinse under cold water. Dry the prawns and cover them with the lemon juice. Allow to stand for several hours. Drain the prawns and discard lemon juice. Place the olive oil in a bowl, add the prawns and toss thoroughly so they are well coated and glossy. Remove the prawns and place on a serving dish, sprinkle with dried tarragon, salt and freshly ground black pepper to taste. Peel and finely slice the onion, separating the rings. Place on top of the prawns and serve immediately.

NOTE: This salad can also be used as hors d'oeuvres, served on toothpicks.

EGG AND POTATO SALAD

6 fresh eggs
8 large potatoes
225 g sour cream
2 egg yolks
25 ml lemon juice
25 g parsley
2 teaspoons paprika
salt and white pepper

serves 4

Hard-boil the eggs by placing them in a saucepan with 575 ml of boiling water. Allow to boil for 7 minutes, remove from heat and let the eggs cool down in the same water. When quite cold, peel off the shells, rinse under cold water, dry and chop each egg into 4 pieces. Peel and wash the potatoes, place in a saucepan and cover with cold water. Bring to the boil, cook for 10 minutes then remove from heat. Let stand for 15 minutes, drain and dice the potatoes. Place the sour cream in a mixing bowl and beat in the egg yolks. When smooth, beat in the lemon juice. Add parsley, paprika, salt and pepper to taste. Put the eggs and potatoes in a salad bowl and pour the sour cream mixture on top. Stir thoroughly, making sure all pieces are covered and refrigerate for 1 hour before serving.

TOMATO AND CUCUMBER SALAD

4 large tomatoes
2 cucumbers
6 spring onions
2 shallots
150 ml yoghurt
1 teaspoon cayenne pepper
1 pinch basil
salt and pepper

serves 4

Wash tomatoes and cut into wedges. Peel cucumber and slice. Chop the spring onions and peel and slice shallots. Place the above ingredients into a salad bowl. Combine the yoghurt, cayenne pepper, basil, salt and pepper to taste, then pour over the vegetables making sure all are properly coated. Refrigerate for 1 hour before serving.

HOT CHILLI SALAD

225 ml olive oil
3 cloves garlic
25 ml lime juice
2 teaspoons salt
1 onion
10 spring onions
1 cucumber
1 tomato
1 red capsicum
1 green capsicum
2 red chillies
2 green chillies
25 g parsley
6 dashes tabasco
1 teaspoon cayenne pepper
freshly ground black pepper
125 g dessicated coconut
1 hard-boiled egg
300 g shredded lettuce

serves 4

Place olive oil in a bowl and add crushed garlic, lime juice and salt. Allow to 'steep' for 1 hour. Peel and grate the onion, chop spring onions finely using white stalk or bulb and about 25 mm of the green stalk, peel and finely dice cucumber, peel and chop tomato, finely dice capsicum and chillies. Place these ingredients in a separate bowl and add parsley, cayenne pepper, tabasco and freshly ground black pepper. Cut the hard-boiled egg in half, remove yolk and force through a very fine sieve with a wooden spoon. Repeat process with egg whites and reserve. Pour the oil mixture onto vegetables and mix thoroughly. Place the shredded lettuce in a salad bowl and pour the salad on top. Sprinkle egg whites and yolks over the top together with the coconut. Serve immediately.

NOTE: If an extra-hot salad is preferred, add more chillies, tabasco and cayenne pepper.

JULIUS SALAD

2 heads romaine or cos lettuce
3 slices thick bread
2 cloves garlic
150 ml olive oil
1 teaspoon dry mustard
1 teaspoon tarragon vinegar
100 ml lemon juice
2 eggs
4 bacon rashers
6 anchovy fillets
200 g parmesan cheese
100 g almonds
salt and pepper

serves 6

Peel and crush the garlic into a wooden bowl, pour olive oil into the bowl and mix well with the garlic. Leave to 'steep' for several hours. Strain off oil and reserve garlic. Wash and drain the lettuce leaves, pat dry and place leaves in a plastic bag and put in the refrigerator to crisp. Make a vinaigrette by beating together the oil, mustard powder, vinegar, lemon juice, salt and freshly ground black pepper to taste. When eggs have reached room temperature, gently lower them into 500 ml of rapidly boiling water. Allow the eggs to cook for exactly 1 ½ minutes, remove and place in a bowl of cold water to cool down. Chop the bacon and place in a frying pan together with reserved garlic and fry until crisp and brown. Drain and reserve. Dice the slices of bread and fry in the bacon fat until crisp. Drain and reserve. Take lettuce leaves from the refrigerator and tear leaves into rough pieces. Place in the salad bowl and toss with the vinaigrette until all leaves are nicely coated and glossy. Make a well in the centre and break the coddled eggs into it, whisk slightly with a fork then toss leaves again. Add the bacon, garlic and croutons. Chop the anchovies and almonds and sprinkle over the salad. Top with grated parmesan cheese and serve immediately.

SUMMER COLESLAW

½ head cabbage
2 carrots
1 onion
500 g cooked rice
250 g cooked peas
250 g corn kernels
6 spring onions
6 radishes
1 green capsicum
1 red capsicum
2 cloves garlic
250 g sour cream
50 ml tarragon vinegar
salt and black pepper to taste

serves 6

Wash and pat dry the cabbage leaves, shred finely and place in a large salad bowl. Peel and grate the carrots and onion and add to cabbage. Mix in the cooked rice, peas, corn, sliced spring onions and radishes. Dice the peppers and add to salad. Crush the garlic and mix with the sour cream and tarragon vinegar. When smooth, pour over the salad, toss thoroughly, season to taste with salt and pepper and toss again. Store in refrigerator until ready for use.
NOTE: This dish will keep in the refrigerator for several days.

Summer Coleslaw

GUATEMALA BEEF SALAD

450 g minced beef
225 ml olive oil
3 cloves garlic
1 lime (or lemon)
2 teaspoons salt
1 onion
10 spring onions
1 large cucumber
1 large tomato
50 g red capsicum
2 teaspoons red chillies
1 potato
1 teaspoon parsley
1 teaspoon oregano
2 teaspoons tabasco
1 teaspoon cayenne pepper
black pepper

serves 4

'Dry fry' the beef (do not use any oil or other shortening) over a high heat and continue to cook until all the natural juices have been absorbed and the meat becomes brown and separates easily. Remove from heat and allow to cool, then place in refrigerator. Place the olive oil in an earthenware bowl. Peel and crush the garlic and add to oil with the juice of lime or lemon and salt. Peel and finely chop the onion, spring onions and cucumber, add to oil mixture and toss thoroughly. Finely chop peeled tomato, capsicum and chillies and add to oil. Peel and wash potato, cut in halves and cook for 10 minutes in boiling water. Turn off heat and allow potato to cool, covered, in the water. When cool enough to handle, chop and dice and add to salad. Toss in the parsley, oregano, tabasco, cayenne and black pepper. Set aside to 'steep' for several hours in the refrigerator before serving. Serve in lettuce cups or wrap the mixture in blanched cabbage leaves.

SALAMI SALAD

12 slices hard salami
12 slices Black Forest ham
12 slices metwurst or german
sausage
24 stuffed green olives
50 g cream cheese
25 g caviar
50 g capers

serves 4

Curl the salami around to make cone-shaped, place half a stuffed green olive in the centre and secure with a toothpick. Place in a circle on the outer side of a large flat plate. Make another circle inside with rolled Black Forest ham. Make cones out of the metwurst or german sausage, place a teaspoon of cream cheese inside each one then top with a little caviar and place towards the centre of the plate. Fill the centre of the plate with remaining stuffed green olives and capers. Decorate the edges of the plate with lemon twists, parsley sprigs or slices of hard-boiled eggs. Serve very cold.

THREE BEAN SALAD

1 tin three-bean mix
1 tin kidney beans
1 tin green lima beans
1 onion
2 cloves garlic
1 lemon
1 teaspoon parsley, chopped
1 teaspoon mint, chopped
50 ml olive oil
25 ml tarragon vinegar

serves 4

Open tins and strain off liquid. Place beans in a salad bowl. Peel and grate the onion. Peel and crush the garlic and add to the beans. Extract the juice from the lemon and place in separate bowl together with parsley, mint, olive oil and tarragon vinegar. Beat thoroughly with a wire whisk and when well blended, stir into the bean mixture. Toss thoroughly and serve immediately.

COCONUT SALAD

1 fresh coconut
8 shallots
2 red chillies
1 green chilli
2 teaspoons parsley
3 leaves sweet marjoram,
    chopped

serves 4

Remove flesh from coconut and grate roughly. (If fresh coconut is unobtainable use 225 g dessicated coconut moistened with 50 ml of boiling water). Peel and finely slice the shallots and chillies and add to the coconut mixture. Stir in the parsley and chopped sweet marjoram. Mix thoroughly and serve with curries, meat or chicken dishes.

CHEESE AND AVOCADO SALAD

2 cloves garlic
100 ml peanut or sesame oil
50 ml tarragon vinegar
1 teaspoon dry mustard
1 teaspoon chopped mint
100 g cheddar cheese
100 g gruyère cheese
50 g ementhal cheese
2 avocados
25 ml lemon juice
1 head lettuce
salt and pepper

serves 6

Peel and crush the garlic into a large wooden salad bowl. Add the oil and mix thoroughly, set aside to 'steep' for 20 minutes. Blend the vinegar and mustard powder together and when smooth, beat into the oil and garlic. Stir in the chopped mint and refrigerate the vinaigrette until ready for serving. Cut the three cheeses into 'julienne' strips. Halve the avocados and remove stones. Peel away skin and slice the flesh. Sprinkle with lemon juice to prevent browning. When ready for serving, remove vinaigrette from refrigerator and pour into a jug. Wash the lettuce leaves and pat dry. Tear into bite-sized pieces and place in the salad bowl. Pour a little vinaigrette on the leaves and toss thoroughly so each piece is glossy, add the cheese strips and toss again. Just before serving add the avocados, a little more vinaigrette, salt and pepper to taste. Toss thoroughly once more and serve immediately.

Crabmeat Salad/Green Vegetable Salad

CRABMEAT SALAD

450 g fresh crabmeat
250 g shredded cabbage
250 g shredded lettuce

VINAIGRETTE

250 ml olive oil
125 ml tarragon vinegar
1 clove garlic
25 g parsley
½ teaspoon dried fennel
½ grated onion
salt and pepper to taste

serves 6

Pour the olive oil into a large salad bowl. Crush the garlic and add to oil, mix thoroughly and set aside to 'steep' for several hours. Beat in the vinegar, parsley, fennel, grated onion and salt and pepper. Pour the mixture into a fresh bowl or screwtop jar. Place the shredded cabbage and lettuce in the salad bowl, add the crabmeat and toss thoroughly so they are evenly distributed. Pour some of the vinaigrette mixture over the salad and toss again. Serve immediately.

GREEN VEGETABLE SALAD

½ head lettuce
250 g shredded cabbage
10 spring onions
1 green capsicum
1 stalk celery
125 g cooked peas
225 g cooked green beans (whole)
225 g asparagus

VINAIGRETTE

200 ml olive oil
75 ml wine vinegar
1 teaspoon dried mustard
1 clove crushed garlic
salt and pepper to taste

serves 6

Wash and pat dry the lettuce leaves and tear into bite-sized pieces. Place in a bowl and add the shredded cabbage, chopped spring onions, sliced capsicum, chopped celery and cooked peas. Toss thoroughly. In a separate bowl, mix the mustard powder with a little of the oil until smooth. Slowly beat in the remaining oil and vinegar in alternate streams. Add the crushed garlic, salt and pepper to taste and mix thoroughly. Pour the vinaigrette over the salad, toss again then drain off any excess liquid. Decorate the top of the salad with alternate strips of whole beans and asparagus. Serve immediately.

ESCARGOTS FARCI

24 escargots
275 ml vegetable stock
150 ml red wine
2 teaspoons fine herbs
2 teaspoons sage
25 g butter
50 g flour
6 cloves garlic
1 teaspoon parsley
½ teaspoon dillweed
25 ml cognac

serves 4

Soak the escargots in warm water and a little salt for 1 hour, strain and rinse in fresh cold water. Remove the escargots from their shells, wash shells thoroughly and set aside to drain. Trim the escargots thoroughly and place in a saucepan together with stock, wine, fine herbs and sage. Bring to the boil then reduce heat and simmer for 1½ hours. Blend the butter and flour together until smooth. Peel and crush the garlic and add to the butter together with parsley and dillweed. In each shell, place a teaspoon of cognac then place escargot in the shell. Seal each shell with the butter mixture, place on a plate or shallow dish and bake in the oven at 200°C (gas mark 6) for 25 minutes. Remove from oven, place on escargot plates and serve immediately.

OYSTER MORNAY

225 g boiling oysters
100 ml white wine
500 ml milk
50 g butter
50 g flour
25 ml lemon juice
50 g freshly grated gruyère
    cheese
50 g fresh breadcrumbs
salt and pepper
1 knob additional butter

serves 4

Place oysters in a saucepan with the dry white wine and slowly bring to the boil. Reduce heat and simmer until nearly all the liquid has been absorbed. Remove from heat and lightly mash with a fork. Heat the milk in a saucepan and when just off the boil, remove from heat. Melt the butter in a pan and stir in the sifted flour, cook for 1 minute then remove from heat. Slowly pour in the milk, stirring until smooth, then stir in the lemon juice a little at a time. Add oysters to the sauce and mix thoroughly. Pour the mornay into a flame-proof dish, season to taste with salt and pepper. Sprinkle the cheese and breadcrumbs on top and dot with butter. Either grill the mornay or place it in a hot oven until breadcrumbs are nicely browned. Serve immediately.

CUCUMBER AND PRAWNS WITH BUTTER SAUCE

3 large cucumbers
4 shallots, finely chopped
1 lemon
300 g prawns
25 g parsley
1 teaspoon tarragon
salt and pepper

serves 6

Wash cucumbers and cut in half lengthwise, leaving skins intact. Remove softer flesh from the middle leaving the firmer flesh on the sides and bottoms. Place the flesh in a bowl and mash lightly. Mix in the chopped shallots and the juice of 1 lemon. Shell the prawns and mince them finely, add to cucumber mixture together with parsley and tarragon. Season to taste with salt and pepper then spoon the mixture back into the cucumber shells. Make a butter sauce (refer page 114) and pour over the cucumber. To serve, place on a plate with lettuce cups, tomato halves and hard-boiled egg quarters.

STUFFED AUBERGINES

3 aubergines (eggplant)
salt
1 onion
225 g minced beef
1 teaspoon oregano
1 teaspoon basil
1 red chilli, sliced
50 g grated gruyère
salt and pepper to taste
SAUCE:
25 g butter
25 g flour, sifted
250 ml milk, warmed
50 ml cream
salt and pepper

serves 6

Cut the aubergines in half lengthwise, sprinkle with a generous amount of salt (to extract moisture and tenderise flesh) and set aside for 15 minutes. Place aubergines under a hot grill for 10 minutes then remove flesh, reserving the skins, and chop finely. Peel and grate the onion and add to aubergine flesh. 'Dry fry' the minced beef until all juices are absorbed and the meat is brown and separates easily. Add the meat to aubergines together with oregano, basil, chilli, grated gruyère cheese and mix thoroughly. Season to taste with salt and pepper. Place the mixture back into the reserved skins. To make the sauce, melt the butter and stir in the sifted flour. Cook, stirring, for 1 minute then gradually add the warmed milk, a little at a time and beat until smooth. Reduce the heat and stir in the cream (do not boil). Season to taste and pour the sauce over the aubergines. Place on a baking tray in a moderate oven for 30 minutes. Serve garnished with lettuce, tomato slices and lemon wedges.

MARINATED MUSHROOMS

225 g champignons or cultivated mushrooms
100 g lettuce
100 g cabbage

MARINADE
150 ml soya sauce
150 ml dry white wine
250 ml olive oil
125 ml wine vinegar
25 mm ginger root
3 cloves garlic
1 spanish onion
1 teaspoon fine herbs
50 ml lemon juice
black pepper to taste

serves 6

Mix together the soya sauce, dry white wine, olive oil and vinegar. Peel the ginger root, grate and add to marinade. Crush the garlic, peel and grate the onion, add to marinade together with remaining ingredients. Wipe the champignons (do not wash) with a damp cloth, trim stalks and discard. Finely slice all the champignons except 6 which should be put aside and left whole for garnishing. Add the sliced champignons to the marinade mixture and refrigerate overnight if possible, but full flavour will be reached if made at least 2 or 3 days in advance. To serve, strain champignons and reserve marinade. Finely shred cabbage and lettuce and place in 6 individual entrée glasses. Divide the champignons into 6 equal portions and place on the lettuce and cabbage base. Spoon 3 or 4 teaspoons of the marinade mixture over the top and garnish with a decorated mushroom (see note below) and lemon wedges.

NOTE: To decorate mushrooms, make 10 slices from the centre of the cap to the stalk in a circular movement. Peel skin from every 2nd segment. Place the mushrooms upside down in the marinade mixture and to serve place on top of the prepared dish.
If fresh ginger root is unavailable, use 1 teaspoon of powdered ginger instead.

STUFFED PANCAKES

100 g flour
275 ml milk
2 eggs
1 pinch fine herbs
1 teaspoon paprika
salt to taste

STUFFING
200 g cream cheese
1 packet frozen chopped spinach
  (or 12 fresh leaves)
1 clove garlic
half onion
275 ml chicken stock
150 ml brandy

serves 6

To make the batter, sift flour, salt and paprika together. Make a well in the centre and add egg yolks and whisk briskly. Pour the milk, a little at a time, into the batter and beat until smooth. Set aside for 1 hour then stir in the fine herbs. Melt 25 g of butter in a frying pan and cook pancakes, one at a time, until all the mixture is used up. They should be of a light golden colour on both sides. As each pancake is cooked, stack on a heated plate and keep warm in the oven. If desired, greaseproof paper can be placed between each one to prevent sticking. In a mixing bowl, place the cream cheese and work it with a wooden spoon until soft. Add the crushed garlic, grated onion and spinach and stir until smooth. Place spoonfuls of this mixture in the centre of the pancakes, turn ends in and roll up. Keep warm in the oven. Boil the chicken stock until volume is reduced by half. Heat the brandy, pour it over the pancakes and set alight to flame. Add chicken stock and serve immediately. Garnish with sprigs of watercress or parsley.

Stuffed Pancakes

CRABMEAT COCKTAIL

225 g fresh crabmeat
4 lettuce cups
225 g shredded lettuce
250 ml mustard sauce (see
   page 116)

serves 4

Wash the lettuce and pat dry with a clean cloth. Place the lettuce cups in cocktail glasses and cover with shredded lettuce. Divide crabmeat into 4 equal portions and place on the lettuce bed. Spoon the mustard sauce over the crabmeat and serve immediately, garnished with lemon wedges and parsely sprigs.

CLAMS NOILLY PRAT

1¼ kilos clams
150 ml water
150 ml white wine
2 large onions
25 g parsley
2 teaspoons basil
25 g tomato purée
25 g oil
25 g butter
50 g cooked mashed potato
175 ml Noilly Prat dry
   vermouth
salt and pepper

serves 4

Wash the clams thoroughly and place in a saucepan with water and white wine and cook covered over a high heat to open shells. Shake the pan frequently. When shells are opened, remove clams and drain. Strain the liquid through a muslin cloth and reserve. Discard any unopened clams. Peel and finely dice the onions and mix with parsley, basil and tomato purée. Place oil and butter in a frying pan and gently fry the onion mixture for 2 minutes then add the previously cooked mashed potato. Mix thoroughly and evenly, pour in the Noilly Prat and reserved liquid. Cook for a further 10 minutes. Season to taste with salt and pepper. Put the clams into the sauce and re-heat gently, then transfer to a shallow serving dish, sprinkle with paprika and serve immediately.

SALMON MORNAY

500 g salmon (fresh or tinned)
1 onion, finely sliced
2 tomatoes, skinned and
   chopped
4 shallots, sliced
400 ml béchamel sauce
salt and pepper
25 ml lemon juice
300 g fresh breadcrumbs
2 knobs butter

serves 4

Lightly sauté the onion in a little oil until soft. Flake the flesh of salmon slightly and line a flat casserole dish with alternate layers of fish, onion, tomato and shallots until all have been used up. Pour the béchamel sauce over the top, season to taste with salt, pepper and lemon juice. Sprinkle fresh breadcrumbs over the top and dot with butter. Bake in a moderate oven for 45 minutes or until the breadcrumbs are nicely browned and the mixture is well heated through. Serve immediately, garnished with lemon wedges and parsley sprigs.

MUSSELS MACADAMIA

36 fresh mussels
1 litre boiling water
2 cloves garlic, crushed
1 onion, diced
1 pinch basil
1 pinch thyme
1 pinch marjoram
1 teaspoon mustard seeds
4 whole black peppercorns
75 ml olive oil
225 g macadamia or pine nuts
1 bay leaf
225 ml dry white wine
100 ml béchamel sauce
50 g parsley
salt and pepper to taste

serves 6

Trim, wash and scrape the mussels. To open them, place in rapidly boiling water, shaking pan frequently. When mussels have opened, drain and reserve stock. Discard any mussels which have not opened. Place the crushed garlic, diced onion, basil, thyme, marjoram, mustard seeds, black peppercorns, olive oil and nuts into a liquidiser. Blend until all ingredients are finely ground then place in a saucepan with reserved stock, bay leaf and white wine. Slowly bring to the boil, reduce heat to simmer, cover and cook for 10 minutes. Place reserved mussels into the sauce and cook for a further 5 minutes. Remove bay leaf and discard. Mix the béchamel sauce with a little stock until well blended. Add to sauce but do not boil. When ready to serve, place the mussels into individual bowls and sprinkle with chopped parsley.

SEAFOOD BARQUETTES

12 barquettes (or pastry boats)
150 g prawns or shrimps, minced
75 g clams, minced
75 g mussels, minced
150 g crayfish or lobster meat, minced
100 ml 'béchamel' sauce
2 teaspoons parsley
1 pinch sage
2 teaspoons paprika
salt and pepper to taste

serves 6

Make 12 barquettes or boat-shaped pastry cases out of shortcrust pastry (see page 113) and bake 'blind' for 15 minutes. Using fresh or canned shellfish, mince the flesh finely and mix in with béchamel sauce, parsley and sage. Season to taste with salt and pepper. Spoon this mixture into the barquettes and sprinkle with paprika. Bake in a moderate oven for 15-20 minutes or until the mixture is bubbling slightly. Serve 2 per person on shredded cabbage decorated with mint leaves and lemon twists.

LOBSTER AND AVOCADO COCKTAIL

1 fresh lobster tail (about 375 g)
2 ripe avocados

COCKTAIL SAUCE
250 g cream
25 g tomato purée
25 g chilli sauce
¼ teaspoon tabasco
1 teaspoon worcestershire sauce
25 ml lemon juice
salt and pepper to taste

serves 4

Cut the lobster tail into medallions to serve 4 people. Place in the centre of entrée dishes. Cut the avocados in half, remove the stones then carefully scrape the skin away. Slice the avocados and place in a circle around the lobster tail. Squeeze a little fresh lemon juice on each slice to prevent browning. Whip the cream until quite stiff. Beat in the tomato purée, chilli sauce, tabasco, worcestershire and lemon juice. When smooth, add salt and pepper to taste. Spoon the sauce over the lobster meat and serve immediately.

POTTED SHRIMPS

150 g shrimps
100 g butter
1 pinch tarragon
3 teaspoons parsley
salt and pepper
75 g butter

Using a mortar and pestle, pound the shrimps and butter together until the mixture is smooth. Place shrimps in a bowl and mix in the tarragon, parsley, salt and pepper with a fork. Place the butter in a frying pan and clarify by bringing to the boil. Do not allow the butter to burn. Boil gently until a white foam or scum appears on top. Remove from heat and let the butter settle for a few minutes, then strain through a muslin cloth. Discard the sediment. Pour the clarified butter into individual bowls and refrigerate for 15 minutes. Spoon the pounded shrimps on top of the clarified butter, pressing until firm and refrigerate for several hours before serving. When ready for use, turn the potted shrimps out onto small flat plates decorated with shredded lettuce, parsley sprigs and lemon wedges. Serve with fingers of toast.

Lobster and Avocado Cocktail/Potted Shrimps

CURRIED EGGS IN CREAM SAUCE

9 eggs
25 g curry powder
25 g butter
2 teaspoons parsley
salt and peper
SAUCE:
25 g butter
25 g flour
200 g additional butter
50 g curry powder
6 spring onions
2 egg yolks, beaten
75 ml cream
salt
cayenne pepper

serves 6

Gently lower the eggs into a saucepan of cold water and bring to the boil. Allow to boil rapidly for 10 minutes. Turn off heat and leave eggs to stand for a further 10 minutes. Strain off water and soak the eggs in fresh cold water. When cool enough to handle, peel off the shells, rinse in cold water and pat dry. Cut eggs lengthwise and carefully remove the yolks, reserving the whites. Place the yolks in a bowl and mash thoroughly. Mix in the curry powder, butter, parsley and season to taste with salt and black pepper. Spoon the mixture back into the egg whites, and place in a shallow gratin dish. Make the sauce by melting the butter in a saucepan and stir in the flour. Cook for 1 minute without browning. Beat in the additional butter a little at a time and whisk until the mixture is smooth and creamy. Add the beaten egg yolks and cook over a gentle heat without boiling until mixture thickens slightly. Chop the spring onions and add to sauce. Blend the curry powder with a little cream, remove mixture from heat and stir in the curry and remaining cream. Adjust seasoning. Pour sauce over the eggs and place in a warm oven for 15 minutes or until eggs have heated through. To serve, sprinkle with cayenne pepper.

EGG AND CHILLI FLAN

200 g shortcrust pastry
50 g sour cream
6 eggs
100 g grated coconut
1 red chilli
1 green chilli
4 shallots
75 g cheddar cheese, grated
½ teaspoon tabasco
salt and pepper
cayenne pepper

serves 4

Roll pastry out to 3 mm thickness and line a 23 mm pie plate or flan case. Do not trim pastry. Set aside to allow for shrinkage. Beat the sour cream until it runs smooth, add eggs and mix thoroughly. Stir in the coconut, chopped chillies, sliced shallots, cheddar cheese, tabasco, salt and pepper to taste. Trim the pastry and prick in several places to allow air to escape during cooking. Pour the egg mixture into the pie plate and sprinkle the top with cayenne pepper. Place in a moderately warm oven for 30 minutes or until eggs are quite set. Serve hot or cold as an entrée or main course.

SCRAMBLED EGGS WITH CAVIAR

4 lettuce leaves
4 small tomatoes
6 large fresh eggs
50 g butter
25 g chopped chives
25 g chopped parsley
100 ml cream
75 g caviar
salt and pepper

serves 4

Wash and pat dry the lettuce leaves and shred finely. Place in the refrigerator until ready for use. Cut tops off the tomatoes and scoop out the seeds and flesh. Cut a thin slice from the bottom of tomatoes so they will stand on a plate and place in a warm oven to heat through. Beat the eggs until smooth, then strain through a fine sieve. Fill the bottom of a double saucepan with 150 ml of water, bring to the boil, then reduce heat so that the water is only just off the boil. Put butter in the top of the saucepan and place over the steaming water. When butter has melted, add the beaten eggs and stir continually with a wooden spoon until the mixture starts to set. Remove from heat and stir in chopped chives, parsley and cream. Return to heat and continue to cook, stirring until the eggs start to 'scramble'. Season to taste with salt and pepper, remove from heat and place spoonfuls of the egg mixture into the tomatoes, top with caviar and serve on a bed of shredded lettuce with slices of lemon and sprigs of parsley.

MARINATED HERRINGS

3 herrings, smoked
1 teaspoon thyme
1 teaspoon rosemary
1 teaspoon sweet marjoram
1 carrot
2 onions
4 bay leaves
225 ml olive oil
8 whole black peppercorns
1 clove garlic

serves 6

Remove fillets from herrings, making sure all bones are removed, and scrape away the skin. Cut each fillet in half lengthwise to make 12 pieces. Make a bouquet garni by placing the thyme, rosemary and sweet marjoram in a muslin cloth and secure top with cotton or string. Scrape skin from carrot and slice thinly. Peel onions, cut into rounds and separate the rings. Place 2 bay leaves in the bottom of a casserole dish; place layers of herrings, carrot slices, oil and peppercorns on top until all the ingredients are used up. Peel and crush the garlic and place in the casserole. Add the bouquet garni and the last 2 bay leaves, cover the top with greaseproof paper and leave to stand at room temperature overnight. To serve, drain the herrings on kitchen paper, place on a bed of shredded lettuce, sprinkle with chopped parsley and top with prepared onion rings.

NOTE: If herrings are unavailable, use packaged kippers.

STUFFED SMOKED SALMON CONES

12 slices smoked salmon
225 g philadelphia cheese
3 teaspoons capers
3 teaspoons onion, grated
3 teaspoons egg white and yolk
1 teaspoon parsley, chopped
1 teaspoon lemon juice
black pepper
50 g caviar
6 stuffed green olives

serves 6

Place the slices of smoked salmon on a flat surface and trim to make square. Reserve the trimmings. Place the cheese in a bowl and work it with a wooden spoon until it is soft and smooth. Mix in the capers, onion, minced egg white and yolk, parsley, lemon juice, salmon trimmings and black pepper to taste. When well blended, place spoonfuls of this mixture on the smoked salmon, leaving about 25 mm free at the top of the cone. Roll up into a cone-shape and place one teaspoon of the caviar in the top of the opening in each cone. Place half a stuffed green olive in the centre of the caviar. Serve 2 cones per person, garnished with lemon wedges and sprigs of fresh parsley.

DEVILLED CRAB

575 g crabmeat
50 g butter
75 g flour
425 ml milk or stock
1 egg yolk
25 ml worcestershire sauce
1 onion
½ teaspoon marjoram
1 pinch cayenne pepper
25 ml lemon juice
175 g breadcrumbs
salt and pepper

serves 6

Make a roux by melting the butter in a saucepan, sift in the flour and stir over a moderate heat for 1 minute. Remove from heat and slowly add the milk or stock, a little at a time and stirring to prevent lumps. When smooth add the beaten egg yolk and return pan to heat. Stir until slightly thickened but do not allow to boil. Strain through a fine sieve and return mixture to a clean pan. Add worcestershire sauce and mix thoroughly. Peel the onion and place in boiling water for a few minutes to scald. Dice finely and add to sauce together with marjoram, cayenne, lemon juice, salt and pepper to taste. Return to heat and add crabmeat. Simmer for a further 10 minutes or until the crabmeat is hot. Fill ramekin dishes with this mixture, sprinkle with fresh breadcrumbs, dot with butter and place under a hot grill until the top turns a nice golden brown. Serve immediately.
NOTE: If available, use crab shells in place of ramekin dishes.

Devilled Crab

BRAIN PATTIES

500 g calf's or sheep's brains
700 ml veal stock
25 ml vinegar
2 teaspoons lemon juice
75 g mushrooms
25 g butter
8 spring onions
2 teaspoons parsley
salt and pepper
flour
egg yolks
breadcrumbs
oil for deep frying

serves 4

Soak the brains in cold water to which a little salt has been added, for 1 hour. Drain, remove skin and blood tissues, then pat dry. Simmer the brains in veal stock, vinegar and lemon juice for 20 minutes. Drain the brains then place them in a bowl of cold fresh water until cool. Remove brains, pat dry, place in a dish and mash until smooth. Trim and wipe mushrooms and dice finely. Heat butter in a frying pan and gently sauté the mushrooms until soft. Peel, wash and finely slice the spring onions and add to brains together with mushrooms, parsley, salt and pepper to taste. When well mixed, form the brains into patties, dip in flour, egg yolks then breadcrumbs and put aside for 30 minutes in the refrigerator to 'set'. Heat the oil in a deep frying pan and when a blue smoke appears, gently lower the patties into the oil, 2 or 3 at a time and fry until breadcrumbs turn a golden brown. Remove and drain on kitchen paper and place in a low oven until ready for use. Serve on a bed of fresh spinach leaves, creamed potatoes and carrots in honey.

POTTED HARE

450 g hare meat
1 teaspoon allspice
1 bouquet garni
3 rashers streaky bacon
1 strip lemon peel
½ teaspoon black pepper
1 teaspoon salt
1 pinch cayenne pepper
100 g 'clarified butter'

serves 4

Cut the hare meat into very small pieces. Place in an earthenware dish on a layer of bacon, allspice, bouquet garni and lemon rind. Cover and place in a pan of boiling water and cook in the oven for 30 minutes. Remove hare meat (discard any bones) and force through a mouli or use a liquidiser to mince. Add salt and pepper to taste. Pound this mixture well until quite smooth, adding the pan juices a little at a time, and mix in the cayenne pepper. Pour the 'clarified butter' into individual dishes and press the hare mixture into each one, making sure they are patted down sufficiently. Refrigerate for at least 3 hours before serving then turn out onto plates decorated with lettuce leaves, sprigs of parsley and chopped spring onions.

CALF'S LIVER WITH LEEK SAUCE

750 g calf's liver
50 g butter
50 ml brandy
575 ml chicken stock
4 leeks
100 g mushrooms
50 ml oil
2 teaspoons sugar
50 ml dry sherry
2 teaspoons parsley
25 g flour
25 g butter
salt and pepper

serves 6

Wash, trim and wipe dry the liver; divide into 6 portions. Sprinkle with salt and freshly ground black pepper and set aside to 'steep' for 15 minutes. Melt the butter in a frying pan then gently sauté the liver, sealing pieces well on both sides. Pour the brandy over, cook for 30 seconds then set alight and flame. When flame dies out, add chicken stock, bring to the boil then transfer liver, pan juices and stock to a casserole dish and cook in a low oven for 30 minutes. Wash and trim the leeks and mushrooms and slice finely. Using a clean frying pan, heat the oil then fry the leeks and mushrooms until soft but not brown. Sprinkle vegetables with sugar then add sherry and parsley, reduce heat to very low and cook for 3 minutes. Make a 'beurre-manié' by kneading the flour and butter together. When well blended, drop a teaspoonful at a time into the vegetable sauce and stir until thickened. Remove liver from casserole, drain and place on a serving dish. Pour leek sauce over and serve immediately.

RIS DE VEAU AUX AMANDES

2 pairs calf's sweetbreads
60 g butter
225 g champignons/mushrooms
100 ml brandy/cognac
100 ml cream
1 small can truffles
salt and pepper to taste
25 g flour

DEVILLED ALMONDS
175 g almonds
25 g butter
salt

serves 4

Soak the sweetbreads in cold water for 2 hours, changing the water several times. Put the sweetbreads in a pan of cold water and bring to the boil, reduce heat and simmer for 1 minute then remove from heat and plunge them into fresh cold water. Remove membranes and blood tissues, pat dry and slice very thinly. Heat the butter in a heavy-based pan and add the sweetbreads. Sauté until golden brown (approximately 10 minutes). Wipe and trim mushrooms and slice finely. Add to sweetbreads and sauté until soft. Pour cognac over and flame. Season to taste with salt and pepper. Strain off any excess cognac and place sweetbreads and mushrooms on a warm serving dish. Heat truffles in the cream over a very low heat. Do not boil. Mix the flour with a little water or milk and when smooth mix into the cream and stir until sauce has thickened slightly. Pour sauce over the sweetbreads. Place the almonds in a bowl and pour over boiling water. Leave to soak for 5 minutes, drain and rinse under cold water. Remove skins and split the almonds. Slice into slivers. Heat the butter in a frying pan, sprinkle with salt and fry the almonds, shaking the pan frequently and stirring continuously until they are golden brown in colour. Drain and serve sprinkled over the sweetbreads.

Main Courses

The main course is exactly what it says. There are so many exciting things which one can do with food. A simple dish can be become a gastronomical delight with the careful use of herbs, spices and marinades.

The presentation of a meal is all-important and care must be taken when serving food, that plates are not heavily over-loaded — there is nothing more off-putting than to see a plate mounded with food and to have your guests wondering if they can do justice to the serving or if they will offend the hostess by having to leave half the meal. Small servings are far more desirable and two or three well presented vegetable dishes are better than four or five dishes which can only serve to detract from the main ingredient.

Table settings depend on the type of meal being served and the guests invited. Informal entertaining can be just as much fun as formal dining. If a formal setting is used, keep the table simple and don't overdo it by displaying all your silver and crystal. Don't overcrowd the table — make certain your guests have enough room to eat comfortably and to be able to select freely from the table. Decorations should be kept to a minimum and a single centre candle is more elegant than a candelabra or flower arrangement. Always use white linen in formal dining.

Informal settings should be basically simple in layout. Use plain or coloured crockery and select plain cutlery, glassware and condiment containers. If coloured or floral linen is being used, make sure it doesn't clash with the plates. A small arrangement of flowers on the table is acceptable but candles can be used if preferred.

Lighting of the room should be adequate for guests to see what they are eating and drinking, but not so bright that it is blinding. A medium dim light is ideal, or one main light and table candles.

Buying Food:

If using cheaper cuts of meat, make sure they are marinated or cooked carefully and long enough to become succulent and tender. The delicate flavour of more expensive cuts can be ruined by overdoing the use of herbs and spices and can become tough with the wrong preparation and cooking technique. When buying meat, do it personally so you can see what you are getting. If possible, always buy fresh meat — this is sometimes difficult, especially in countries where the majority of meat is imported and the largest selection is all frozen. Once the meat has been frozen it can be difficult to tell what the quality is like so look for meat which is not covered in frost and you can see the grain and colour quite clearly. Any meat which has brown spots on it (freezer-burn) means it has been frozen for too long. When buying fresh meats, look for the following:-

Beef:	Clear, bright red flesh with pale, firm fat. The best cuts should have a certain amount of fat on them. If fat is very yellow it is a good indication that the meat is from an older beast and will require longer and more careful cooking than younger meats. The meat in older beasts will be very dark red.
Veal:	Very pale pink flesh and white firm fat. There will be very little fat on veal. If colour is light red with firm white or yellow fat, the meat is more likely to be beef and not veal. The cooked flesh of milk-fed veal is white.
Lamb:	The meat is usually dull in colour with white firm fat. Mutton is dark in colour and with longer and more careful cooking, can make a very tasty meal.
Pork:	Firm pale pink flesh and white fat. As pork can be harmful if undercooked, make sure it is well done and never served rare.
Poultry:	Look for birds which are plump and whitish in colour. Yellow skin on chicken and turkey indicates older birds or 'boilers'. Duck and goose are flat-breasted birds whereas chicken and turkey are high breasted. They should be chosen accordingly. If a chicken's breast is flat, it means the bone has been broken or the bird has been frozen and de-frosted.

When buying vegetables, choose those which are in season as they will be fresher, more flavoursome and nourishing.

It is helpful for the hostess to be able to prepare some, if not all, the meal in advance. There are enough last minute preparations to be made without having to spend long periods of time in the kitchen in between courses. Most of the recipes on the following pages have been designed so they can be prepared or made from one to five days in advance, either by marinating or freezing.

Wines and Liqueurs:

I am a great believer in drinking what I like — not what I'm told I should like because it's a more expensive wine or that red wine should be served with red meats, white wine with white meats and fish, and champagne with cheese. Some of the less exclusive wines available today are equally as palatable with certain dishes as expensive wines can be, and for everyday use, it is more sensible and economical to choose a reliable wine and keep the better quality wines for special entertaining.

I have made recommendations for the choice of wines with recipes which I feel are complementary to the ingredients. This is a guide only. It is usual to offer your guests both red and white wine so they can select their preference.

It is customary to serve coffee after the meal with port or liqueurs. Again guests should be asked their preference as some may decide to stay with wine alone. In this day and age there are no set rules — drink what you enjoy and enjoy what you drink.

'Bon Appetit'

FROGS' LEGS IN WHITE SAUCE

36 frogs' legs
flour seasoned with salt, pepper
  and paprika
50 g butter
3 cloves garlic
25 g flour
100 ml white wine
100 ml cream

MARINADE
200 ml white wine
100 ml oil
50 ml lemon juice
1 dash tabasco
3 dashes worcestershire sauce
1 bay leaf
3 cloves garlic
salt and pepper

serves 6

Trim and wipe the frogs' legs. Place all marinade ingredients in an earthenware bowl and whisk until blended. Add the legs and set aside for between 30 minutes and 24 hours. The longer they marinate, the better the flavour. When ready for use, remove legs and pat dry. Strain the marinade mixture and reserve 75 ml for the sauce. Roll frogs' legs in seasoned flour. Melt the butter in a frying pan and add the crushed garlic and legs. Cook until the meat is golden brown, drain and place on a warm serving dish. Stir the flour into butter and garlic and cook for 1 minute. Remove from heat and stir in the reserved marinade mixture and white wine. When smooth return to heat and cook until thickened slightly. Remove from heat and stir in the cream, adjust seasoning and pour sauce over the frogs' legs. Sprinkle with parsley and serve with duchesse potatoes, mushrooms and tomatoes.

FRIED FROGS' LEGS

36 frogs' legs
1 ½ litres chicken stock
1 onion
1 carrot
1 stalk celery
1 bay leaf
6 peppercorns
½ onion, grated
2 cloves garlic
2 teaspoons parsley
25 g fresh breadcrumbs
salt and pepper
3 egg yolks, beaten
breadcrumbs
oil for frying

serves 6

Trim and wipe the frogs' legs and place in a saucepan with chicken stock. Peel and quarter the onion, slice the carrot and celery and add to stock together with bay leaf and peppercorns. Poach gently for 20 minutes, remove from heat and allow to cool. When cold drain the legs and pat dry. Remove flesh from bones and mince or shred finely. Place meat in a bowl and mix in the grated onion, garlic, parsley, breadcrumbs and seasoning. Bind the mixture with 1 beaten egg yolk. Mould this mixture back onto the bones so they resemble the original frogs' legs. Dip into beaten egg yolks then roll in breadcrumbs until well coated. Refrigerate to 'set' legs for 1 hour. When ready for use, deep fry until golden brown and serve immediately with french fries, green peas and lemon wedges.

Wine: Light-bodied red. Médoc, Beaujolais or Cabernet.

SNAILS COCOTTE

48 snails

1 carrot

1 onion

1 teaspoon thyme

1 teaspoon parsley

1 bay leaf

1 teaspoon rock salt

1 litre water

3 cloves garlic

50 ml dry white wine or sherry

75 g shallots

2 cloves

100 ml cream

salt and pepper

50 g chopped parsley

serves 4

To prepare snails, wash thoroughly in 425 ml cold water and 25 ml vinegar. Place snails and liquid in a saucepan, bring to the boil then remove from heat and leave to stand for 10-15 minutes. Strain snails and place in cold water until cool. Remove the snails from their shells and trim away membranes. Place the cleaned snails in a saucepan with sliced carrot, onion, thyme, parsley, bay leaf and rock salt. Cover with 1 litre cold water and simmer for 1½-2 hours. Drain, reserving stock, and set aside the snails and vegetables. Reduce the quantity of stock by two-thirds by boiling rapidly with the lid off, lower heat when sufficiently reduced and add the crushed garlic and white wine or sherry, chopped shallots and cloves. Simmer for 15 minutes then put the snails and vegetables back into stock and cook for a further 5 minutes. Remove from heat and slowly stir in the cream. Season to taste with salt and black pepper and sprinkle the top with chopped parsley. Serve immediately.

Wine: Dry White. Graves or Pouilly-Fuissé

Steamed Ginger Fish/Smoked Cod a la Crème

STEAMED GINGER FISH

1 whole or 2 small fish (perch,
   turbot, whiting, mullet etc)
50 g butter
8 shallots
50 mm piece ginger root
25 ml soya sauce
225 ml dry white wine
1 lemon, juiced
9 spring onions
575 ml fish stock
50 g flour
25 g ginger powder
50 g butter
50 g chopped parsley

serves 4

Scale, gut and wash fish thoroughly. Make several small cuts on either side of fish and sprinkle with salt. Leave to 'steep' for 15 minutes. Line a shallow pan with butter. Peel and slice shallots, peel and grate the ginger root. Place on top of butter together with soya sauce and dry white wine. Place the whole fish on top of this mixture and sprinkle with the juice of a lemon and 'julienne' cut spring onions, cover and bake in a moderate oven for 10 minutes. Place the fish stock in a saucepan and boil rapidly until stock is reduced by two-thirds. Pour the stock over the fish, re-cover and continue to steam in the oven for a further 10 minutes or until the flesh has turned opaque in colour and flakes easily with a fork. Place the fish on a large serving plate, cover with the shallots and ginger. Blend the flour, ginger powder and butter together and place drops into the stock, a little at a time and stir until the mixture thickens slightly. Pour the sauce into a warmed gravy boat and serve separately. Just prior to serving, sprinkle the fish with freshly chopped parsley.

SMOKED COD A LA CREME

675 g smoked cod fillets
575 ml fish stock
1 bouquet garni
225 ml dry white wine
75 g plain flour
75 g butter
300 ml milk
50 g grated gruyère cheese
300 ml cream
50 g parsley, chopped
salt and pepper to taste

serves 6

Trim the fillets and cut into bite-sized pieces. Place the fish stock in a large saucepan and add the bouquet garni and cod. Simmer for 15 minutes, remove cod and reserve. Reduce the stock by half by boiling rapidly with the lid off. When liquid is reduced, remove the bouquet garni and discard. Add white wine and reduce heat to simmer. Blend the flour and butter together to make a beurre-manié. Remove stock from heat and slowly drop teaspoonfuls into the liquid, stirring until smooth. Return saucepan to heat and stir until the mixture has thickened. Add the grated gruyère cheese, stirring until melted. Reduce heat to very low and slowly stir in the cream. Add smoked cod and season to taste with salt and white pepper. Just before serving, sprinkle with chopped parsley. Serve with creamed potatoes and fresh green beans.

Wine: Dry white. Pieroth-trocken,
           Nussdorfer Herrenberg.

SEAFOOD CASSEROLE WITH SAVOURY RICE

100 g prawns
100 g oysters or mussels
75 g sole
75 g cod
100 g crayfish tail
1 onion
1 carrot
25 ml olive oil
3 bay leaves
8 whole black peppercorns
1 teaspoon dillweed
1 teaspoon cayenne pepper
1 teaspoon turmeric
1 litre fish stock
50 g butter
50 g flour
100 ml milk
salt and white pepper
75 g grated cheddar cheese

serves 6

If using live shellfish, plunge the prawns and crayfish into rapidly boiling water, boil for 5 minutes then reduce heat and simmer for 3 minutes. Strain and set aside to cool down. Clean and wipe the sole and cod, remove skin and fillet the fish. Cut fillets into bite-sized chunks. Peel and slice the onion and carrot. Melt the oil in a frying pan and lightly sauté the vegetables until soft. Shell the prawns. Remove meat from crayfish by cutting the under-side of tail with a sharp knife or scissors, starting from the head and working towards the tail. Then gently pull the flesh away and cut into chunks. Line a casserole dish with layers of seafood, vegetables, bay leaves, peppercorns and a pinch of dillweed, cayenne and turmeric until all ingredients are used up. Pour stock over, cover casserole and cook in a moderate oven for 30 minutes. Melt the butter in a pan and stir in the flour. Cook for 1 minute then remove from heat and stir in the milk and a little of the hot casserole liquid, stirring all the time to prevent lumps. Pour the sauce over the seafood and season to taste with salt and white pepper. Sprinkle the top with grated cheese and place under a hot grill until the cheese bubbles and starts to turn golden brown. Serve immediately with savoury rice (see recipe below).

SAVOURY RICE

475 g long-grain rice
50 g butter
chicken stock to cover
1 small green capsicum
1 small red capsicum
6 spring onions
black pepper

serves 6

Melt the butter in a frying pan and cook the raw rice until it is a pale golden colour. Transfer to a saucepan and cover with stock to approximately 25 mm above the rice level. Slowly bring to the boil then reduce heat slightly and allow rice to cook until all the liquid has been absorbed. Cut the capsicums into large dice, wash and slice the spring onions. Place the rice into a warm serving dish and mix in the vegetables. Season with black pepper and serve immediately as above.

Wine: Dry white. Chablis, Muscadet or Riesling.

SOLE PAUPIETTES VICTORIA

8 fillets of sole
225 g lobster meat
½ bottle white wine
½ bottle champagne
1 teaspoon tarragon
25 g parsley
25 g chopped chives
50 g butter
50 g flour
salt and pepper to taste

serves 4

If using a live lobster, firstly plunge it into rapidly boiling water and boil for 1 minute, add ½ a bottle of dry white wine, reduce heat and simmer for 7 minutes. Remove lobster and reserve stock, shell the lobster and cut the tail in half lengthwise. Reserve one half and chop the other half finely, mix in ½ a teaspoon of tarragon, the parsley, chives, salt and pepper. If mixture is too dry, 'bind' with a little beaten egg yolk and flour. Wash and wipe the sole fillets and place on a board, skin side up. Either pipe or place spoonfuls of the lobster mixture in the centre of the fillets, roll up and secure with cotton. Place the reserved stock over a high heat and boil until 225 ml remains. Reduce heat to low and add ½ a bottle of champagne. Place the paupiettes in the stock and poach until the flesh turns opaque in colour and the flesh flakes easily with a fork. Remove from pan and place on a serving dish. Keep warm. Make a beurre-manié by blending the butter and flour together. Place small drops into the stock and stir until smooth. When mixture thickens, reduce heat and add the remaining ½ teaspoon of tarragon, salt and pepper to taste. Roughly chop the remaining half lobster tail and add to the sauce. Cook for 5 minutes then pour over the sole paupiettes. Serve immediately.

Wine: Dry White. Chassagne-Montrachet, Pouilly-Fumé, Chablis.

POACHED TROUT WITH MUSTARD SAUCE

6 small fresh trout (or 3 large)

cold water to cover

1 onion

1 carrot

1 stalk celery with leaf end

1 lemon

1 bay leaf

6 whole black peppercorns

1 teaspoon dillweed

1 teaspoon rock salt

½ teaspoon tarragon

400 ml mustard sauce (refer page 116)

110 g devilled almonds

serves 3

Wash and clean the trout, pat dry and place in a deep pan. Cover with cold water to approximately 25 mm above the fish. Peel and slice onion, carrot and celery. Add to trout together with sliced lemon, bay leaf, peppercorns, dillweed, salt and tarragon. Cover pan and slowly bring to the boil. When water is boiling rapidly, remove pan from the heat and allow to cool for 15 minutes. Remove trout from pan and fillet the fish carefully. Place the fillets on a serving dish and keep warm in a low oven. Place the blanched, sliced almonds in a shallow pan with a little butter and salt. Fry over a medium heat, stirring continually to prevent burning, until the almonds turn a golden brown in colour. Remove trout from the oven, pour mustard sauce over the top then sprinkle with almonds. Serve immediately.

NOTE: This dish can be served hot (as above) or cold. If serving cold, allow the trout to cool completely in the water before removing then place in the refrigerator until ready for use.

Wine: Mellow white. Sauternes or Vouvray. Dry white. Chablis.

Poached Trout with Mustard Sauce

FISH PATTIES WITH LEMON SAUCE

475 g cooked fish (snapper, cod,
  perch, garoupa)
1 onion, grated
25 mm ginger root, grated
1 teaspoon paprika
1 teaspoon chervil
25 g parsley, chopped
2 potatoes, cooked and mashed
3 egg yolks, beaten
salt and pepper
cornflour
breadcrumbs and sesame seeds
oil for frying

SAUCE
200 ml lemon juice
25 g white sugar
100 ml chicken stock
50 g cornflour

serves 4

Place the cooked and boned fish in a bowl and mash with a fork. Add grated onion and ginger root, paprika, chervil and parsley. Mix thoroughly then add cooked, mashed potatoes. Bind the mixture with a little of the beaten egg yolks and season to taste with salt and pepper. Form the mixture into patties, dip in cornflour then egg yolks and finally into equal proportions of breadcrumbs and sesame seeds mixed together. Press the patties down firmly into shape and fry in a little oil until golden brown on all sides. Drain and place on a serving dish in a moderate oven to keep warm. Place the lemon juice in a saucepan with sugar and stir over a low heat until sugar dissolves. Blend the cornflour with a little of the chicken stock. Add remaining stock to saucepan with lemon juice and when boiling, remove from heat and stir in the cornflour. Pour sauce over the patties and serve immediately.

MACKEREL PIE

4 medium mackerel
1 onion
1 bay leaf
8 black peppercorns
milk to cover
1 pastry case
8 shallots
25 g butter
2 tomatoes
12 button mushrooms
2 teaspoons parsley
1 teaspoon paprika
25 g flour
25 g butter
200 ml milk (used for poaching)
salt and pepper

serves 4

Place the cleaned mackerel in a shallow pan. Peel and slice onion and add to fish together with bay leaf and black peppercorns. Cover with milk and poach fish gently for 10 minutes. Remove fish, strain and reserve 200 ml of milk. Line a pie dish with pastry, trim edges, prick the bottom in several places with a fork and bake 'blind' in a moderate oven for 10 minutes. Remove and set aside to cool. Peel and slice the shallots and sauté for a few minutes in butter until soft but not brown. Slice the tomatoes and mushrooms finely. Remove flesh from fish and place in a bowl. Mash lightly with a fork and mix in the parsley and paprika. Place layers of shallots, tomatoes, mushrooms and fish in the cooked pie case. Mix the flour and butter together and drop spoonfuls into the warm milk. Return to heat and stir until thickened. Do not boil. Season to taste and pour the sauce over the fish. Place lid on pie and secure with egg white. Prick the top of the pie in several places to allow air to escape during cooking, coat top with egg white or milk and bake in a moderate oven for 15 minutes or until pastry is golden brown. Serve immediately, garnished with hard-boiled eggs and lemon wedges.

Wine: Dry or mellow white. Chablis, Pouilly-
         fuissé or Sauternes.

PICKLED FISH

**600 g fish (barramundi, garoupa,
  salmon, cod)**
400 ml dark soya sauce
1 clove garlic, crushed
25 mm ginger root, grated
75 ml olive oil
50 ml dark malt vinegar
50 g honey
50 ml brandy
25 g castor sugar
salt and pepper

UNLEAVENED BREAD
375 g plain flour
2 teaspoons salt
water
butter for frying

serves 4

Combine all ingredients except fish in an earthenware bowl. Cut the raw fish into cubes and place in the pickling mixture. Refrigerate for at least 3 days but longer if possible, turning fish pieces at regular intervals to make sure all are properly pickled. To serve, transfer the fish and pickling liquid to a casserole or serving dish and place in the centre of the table. Each guest uses a lidi stick to spike the fish and transfer to a dinner plate. Serve with fresh green salad and unleavened bread.

Unleavened bread:
Mix the sifted flour and salt together. Pour over enough water to make a stiff dough. Knead the mixture for several minutes then set aside for 30 minutes. Roll dough out to the thickness of pastry and cut circles out, using a saucer as a guide. Fry each one in melted butter, press down firmly with a spatula then flip over and cook the other side. When golden brown, remove from butter, drain and serve while still warm.

GRAVAD LAX
(Salted Salmon)

600 g fresh pink salmon
50 g rock salt
50 g sugar
1 teaspoon black peppercorns
25 ml brandy
25 g dillweed

MUSTARD SAUCE
**Refer page 116 but use dillweed
instead of tarragon.**

serves 6

To remove flesh from salmon, cut along the backbone, remove bones leaving the skin intact. Remove the centre part of salmon fillets and wipe with a clean cloth. Rub the skin and flesh with salt then place 1 fillet, skin side down in an earthenware dish. Add some of the sugar, crushed black pepper, a little brandy and dillweed. Place the other fillet flesh side down and cover skin side with remaining sugar, pepper, brandy and dillweed. Refrigerate for at least 2 days. After 1 day, there should be twice the amount of liquid as before; if this is not so, add more rock salt and a little more brandy. When fish is properly pickled, remove from dish and pat dry. Remove skin and reserve. Slice the salmon thinly and serve with the deep fried skin and mustard sauce.

Wine: Red. Saint-émilion, Beaujolais or Bordeaux.

PRAWN CURRY

1 kilo prawns
4 litres boiling water
1 litre beer
75 g rock salt
75 g fish curry powder (refer glossary)
1 onion
50 mm piece ginger root
5 cloves garlic
1 green chilli
1 red chilli
1 ¼ litres santan (refer glossary)
50 g dessicated coconut
25 ml lemon juice
oil for frying
225 ml natural yoghurt

serves 6

Place the live prawns into a large saucepan of boiling water, add beer and boil for 5 to 8 minutes, depending on the size of prawns. Drain and reserve 225 ml of the stock. Place the unshelled prawns on a plate and coat with rock salt, set aside to 'steep' for several hours. Meanwhile, prepare the vegetables by peeling and grating the onion and ginger root, crush the garlic, chop chillies finely and mix all together. Heat oil in a frying pan and fry the onion mixture until fragrant. Blend the curry powder with the reserved stock and add to onion mixture. Stir over high heat until a red oily film appears on top of the mixture. Remove from heat. Peel the shells from prawns, rinse under clean running water and place in a pan together with the 2nd santan and cook for 15 minutes. Add dessicated coconut and fried curry and onion mixture. Stir for several minutes until blended. Cook for a further 15 minutes then add the 1st santan and lemon juice, bring back to the boil and cook for 5 minutes then reduce heat and simmer again for 20 minutes. Remove from the heat and stir in yoghurt and when smooth keep in a warm place — do not allow to boil. Serve with boiled or saffron rice.

Wine: Rosé. Sancerre Rosé, Cassis.
Red. Beaujolais.

Elizabethan Turkey

ELIZABETHAN TURKEY

6½-kilo turkey
1-kilo chicken
500 g pheasant
100 g wild rice stuffing
275 g sage and onion stuffing
650 g chestnut stuffing
14 rashers bacon
salt and pepper
lard for frying and roasting

serves 8

Total weight of uncooked birds with stuffing is approximately 9 kilos.

Have your butcher bone all 3 birds, including drumsticks. Trim off wings as these can be roasted separately. Clean the insides of birds thoroughly, singe off any fine hairs and pluck out any remaining quills. Wipe skin of birds with a damp cloth and rub inside and out with salt and pepper. Make the wild rice stuffing (recipe opposite) and stuff the pheasant, moulding the breast back into its original shape. Sew up with cotton. Make the sage and onion stuffing (recipe opposite) and place a little inside the chicken. Place the pheasant on top and mould the remaining sage and onion around, again forming its original high-breasted shape, and sew up with cotton. Make the chestnut stuffing (recipe opposite) and place a little in the bottom of the turkey. Place the chicken inside the turkey and place the remaining stuffing around, filling in all gaps. Sew turkey up and mould the breast back into shape. The stuffing should be sufficient to maintain the shape of the turkey. If desired, drumsticks can be removed and roasted with the wings. Truss the turkey and tie with string. Place lard in a roasting dish and place the turkey breast-side up, cover with strips of bacon and roast for 1 hour. Turn the turkey over so that the breast side is facing down. This will ensure that the natural juices will run down into the breast and keep it moist. Cook in a moderate oven for 4 hours, checking at regular intervals to make sure it is not burning. As the heat in different ovens varies, the turkey may be covered with tinfoil for the first 5 hours of cooking. After 5 hours of roasting, remove the bacon strips and turn the bird so it is facing breast-side up, lower heat and cook for a further 3 hours. Increase heat to high for the last 30 minutes. Check to see if the bird is browning too quickly and if so reduce heat accordingly. Test to see if turkey is cooked by placing a fine skewer through the breast near the drumstick so that it goes through all 3 birds. If juice runs clear, turkey is cooked. To carve the cooked turkey, carve downwards from breast to back so that each guest receives slices of turkey, chestnut, chicken, sage and onion, pheasant and wild rice stuffing in uniform slices. The total cooking time is between 8½ and 9 hours. Garnish the turkey with glazed chestnuts, parsley and tomato roses. Serve with cranberry sauce, bread sauce or gravy.

Wine: Red. Saint-émilion, Sparkling Burgundy or Margaux.

WILD RICE STUFFING

100 g wild rice
½ teaspoon mixed herbs
1 teaspoon parsley
1 pinch mace
2 juniper berries, crushed
salt and pepper

Place rice in boiling water and boil for 15 minutes. Reduce heat and simmer for a further 15 minutes (this rice is tougher than the usual variety and takes longer to cook). Strain through a fine sieve and place in a mixing bowl. Stir in the mixed herbs, parsley, mace, crushed juniper berries, salt and pepper to taste. If wild rice is unavailable, use normal rice, fry the raw grains in butter until they are golden brown. Drain and boil as above.

SAGE AND ONION STUFFING

2 large onions
125 g breadcrumbs
100 g chopped beef suet
50 g chopped sage
egg yolk to bind
salt and pepper

Skin the onions and either bake in a hot oven or boil rapidly in chicken stock until medium-soft. Remove and cool. When cool enough to handle, chop finely and mix with the fresh breadcrumbs, grated suet, sage, salt and pepper. Bind with an egg yolk.

CHESTNUT STUFFING

250 g best quality sausage meat
150 g chestnuts
250 ml veal or chicken stock
1 celery leaf
1 bay leaf
25 g parsley
2 teaspoons lemon juice
salt and pepper

Cook chestnuts in stock with celery and bay leaf. When soft (test by placing a skewer through the centre of the nut), remove and mash roughly. Combine the mashed chestnut with forcemeat, parsley, lemon juice, salt and pepper. Mix thoroughly and use as required.

CHICKEN WITH CURRY SAUCE

1 pre-cooked chicken
8 shallots
1 large onion
4 large tomatoes
50 g butter
75 g plain flour
425 ml chicken stock
3 teaspoons curry powder
1 teaspoon turmeric
1 teaspoon chilli powder
1 teaspoon ginger powder
225 ml milk
275 ml cream
3 chopped spring onions
parsley
salt and pepper to taste

serves 4

Dice the pre-cooked chicken meat and place in a casserole dish. Finely chop the onion, slice the shallots and add to chicken. Pour boiling water over the tomatoes to crack skins. Remove skins and roughly chop the flesh. Add to chicken. Place the butter in a frying pan and when melted stir in the flour and cook for 1 minute. Remove from heat and slowly add the chicken stock, stirring continuously to prevent lumps. Blend the curry powder, turmeric, chilli and ginger powder with a little cold water until smooth. Add to thickened stock and cook over a gentle heat for a few minutes. Add milk and cook for a further 5 minutes without boiling. Remove from heat and slowly stir in the cream, add salt and pepper to taste and pour the sauce over the chicken. Cover and cook in a medium oven for 30-45 minutes, adjust seasoning if necessary. Before serving, garnish with chopped spring onions and parsley. Serve with spaghetti, boiled or saffron rice.

Wine: Light-bodied red. Médoc or Beaune. Rosé d'Anjou.

CHICKEN AND MUSHROOM WHEELS

450 g chicken breasts

1 large onion

50 g parsley

1 teaspoon sage

1 egg yolk, beaten

25 g flour

225 g mushrooms

salt and pepper

450 g puff pastry (refer page 112)

1 egg white, beaten

serves 4-6

Finely shred or mince the cooked chicken meat. Peel and finely dice the onion and blanch it in boiling water. Add to chicken. Mix in the parsley, sage, salt and pepper and bind together with beaten egg yolk and flour. Wipe and trim the mushrooms and slice finely. Reserve the trimmings for velouté sauce. Lightly sauté the mushrooms in butter until soft but not browned. Remove from heat, drain and reserve. Roll out pastry to 3 mm thickness and cut into strips approximately 23 cm wide and 30 cm long. Place half the mushrooms along the centre of the pastry then either pipe or place spoonfuls of the chicken mixture on top of the mushrooms to form a roll. Place the remaining mushrooms on top and along the sides of the chicken mixture. Brush a little beaten egg-white along the sides of the pastry, roll up and seal edges. Turn the roll over and seal the ends, trim with a pastry cutter and make several small holes in the pastry to allow air to escape. Bake in a hot oven for 30-45 minutes or until the pastry turns golden brown. If desired, before baking, the pastry can be decorated with leaves or flowers cut from left-over pastry pieces, secured with egg white, then baked as above. To serve, cut the roll into 25 mm 'wheels' and serve hot with velouté sauce (refer page 117).

Wine: Dry White. Graves, Montrachet or Riesling.

Chicken and Mushroom Wheels

MANDARIN DUCK WITH BAMBOO AND SHRIMP

1 large duckling
75 ml corn oil
2 cloves garlic
4 shallots
1 onion
4 spring onions
1¼ litres chicken stock
150 g bamboo shoots
200 g mushrooms
225 g fresh shrimps
3 teaspoons cornflour
6 slices mandarin or orange
50 g parsley
salt and pepper

MARINADE

50 ml soya sauce
100 ml sherry
50 ml brandy (optional)
1 teaspoon M.S.G.
1½ teaspoons brown sugar
1½ teaspoons ginger powder
juice of 4 mandarins or oranges

serves 6

Prepare and clean duck, wipe thoroughly with a damp cloth. Cut the flesh into bite-sized pieces. Place all the marinade ingredients into an earthenware dish and mix thoroughly. Add the duck pieces, making sure all are coated properly and leave to stand for at least 1 hour, but longer if possible. Heat the oil in a frying pan, add meat and fry over a high heat until all pieces are nicely browned and sealed on all sides. The skin should be crisp and if preferred, it can be removed at this stage and served separately. Finely chop the shallots, onion, and garlic and stir-fry over a high heat until soft but not browned. Add stock, bring to the boil then reduce heat and simmer for 10 minutes. Place duck in the stock (skin side up if not removed) and cook for 1½ hours or until duck is tender. Finely slice bamboo shoots, wipe and trim mushrooms and chop roughly. Wash and pat dry the shrimps and combine these ingredients with the duck. Continue to cook for a further 5 minutes. Remove duck pieces and place on a large serving dish. Mix cornflour with a little cold water and add to stock, stirring to prevent lumps, until the mixture thickens. Add salt and pepper to taste and pour the sauce over duck. Toss sliced spring onions on top and decorate the plate with mandarin slices and parsley. Serve with plain boiled or butter rice (refer recipe page 97).

Wine: Red. Margaux, Sparkling Burgundy or Saint-émilion.
White. Riesling or Montrachet.

ROAST HONEY DUCKLING

2-kilo duckling
225 ml soya sauce
100 g honey

STUFFING
4 slices stale bread, crumbed
1 onion
1 pinch basil
1 pinch mixed herbs
1 pinch sage
1 egg yolk
salt and pepper

serves 4

Wipe duckling thoroughly, inside and out. Reserve giblets for gravy. Singe off any fine hairs and pluck out feather quills. Make the stuffing by crumbing the stale slices of bread into a bowl. Peel the onion and place in a saucepan of boiling water for 5 minutes. Remove, and when cool chop finely. Add to breadcrumbs together with basil, mixed herbs, sage, salt and pepper and mix thoroughly. Bind with the beaten yolk of an egg. Stuff the duckling and truss. Coat the skin with soya sauce and honey and let the bird hang in a draught for 45 minutes or longer if possible. Prick the skin of the duckling all over to allow fat to run freely during cooking. Coat with soya sauce again then stand bird on a rack in a baking dish lined with tinfoil (to prevent honey from burning the pan) and roast in a moderate oven for 30 minutes or spit roast for the same length of time. Remove bird from heat and coat once again with soya sauce and honey. Re-prick the skin and return bird to oven. Continue basting with soya sauce and honey throughout cooking, remembering to re-prick the skin each time as the honey will block the holes. Allow 25 minutes per ½-kilo plus 25 minutes extra cooking time, or 15 minutes per ½-kilo and 15 minutes extra if liked rare. The ideal way of cooking this dish is on a spit as the fat runs more freely and the heat is distributed more evenly thus preventing burning which will occur in the oven. To make the gravy, wash and wipe the giblets and place in a saucepan of water or stock. Allow to boil for 15 minutes then reduce heat to simmer and continue cooking for 30 minutes longer. Remove giblets. Reduce the liquid quantity by two-thirds then strain liquid through a fine sieve. Return stock to a clean pan. Add some of the pan juices and thicken with beurre-manié (refer glossary). Serve the gravy separately in a gravy boat so the duck skin does not lose its crispness. To carve the duckling, make an incision down the breastbone from head to tail then carve downwards from breast to back in strips. Serve with roast potatoes, carrots and spinach.

Wine: Red. Margaux or Sparkling Burgundy.
White. Riesling or Montrachet.

Roast Honey Duckling

STUFFED QUAIL CASSEROLE

8 quails
16 rashers streaky bacon
50 g butter

MARINADE
225 ml dry sherry
100 ml port
1 teaspoon marjoram
1 teaspoon basil
1 bay leaf
8 juniper berries, crushed
275 ml red wine

STUFFING
3 slices stale bread
1 onion
1 teaspoon mixed herbs
½ teaspoon thyme
½ teaspoon coriander
1 egg yolk to bind

SAUCE
575 ml game stock
125 ml madeira
100 ml marinade mixture
50 g flour
50 g butter

serves 4

Combine all the marinade ingredients together. Place prepared quails in this mixture and allow to stand for 1 or 2 days, turning birds at regular intervals to make sure all parts are evenly marinated. Make the stuffing by crumbing the stale bread. Poach the onion in milk until tender, strain, chop finely and add to breadcrumbs. Mix in the herbs and bind together with egg yolk. Season to taste with salt and pepper. Remove quails from the marinade and pat dry. Cut birds in half. Heat the butter in a frying pan and brown the quails. Drain and place on a chopping board. Fill the breast with stuffing, wrap each half with 2 rashers of bacon and place in casserole dish with 575 ml game stock. Cook in a moderate oven for 10 minutes. Remove quails and keep warm on a serving dish. Using stock which birds were cooked in, add madeira and strained marinade mixture. Bring to the boil and cook until liquid is reduced by half. Make a beurre-manié by kneading the flour and butter together, drop teaspoonfuls into the hot stock and stir until thickened and smooth. Pour sauce over the quails and serve immediately allowing 4 pieces (2 birds) per person.

Wine: Red. Margaux, Beaune or Hermitage.

PHEASANT CASSEROLE

2 pheasants
100 g flour
salt and pepper
fat or lard for frying
225 g mushrooms
4 rashers streaky bacon
4 green peppers
575 ml game stock
250 ml port or dry red wine
50 g parsley

serves 4

Joint the birds and wipe inside and out. Sift the flour, salt and pepper together. Dip the birds into the seasoned flour making sure all pieces are properly coated. Heat the fat in a heavy-based frying pan and sauté the birds until golden brown. Drain on kitchen paper and place in a casserole dish. Trim and wipe the mushrooms and slice finely. Chop the bacon into small pieces and dice the green peppers. Place mushrooms, bacon and peppers in the casserole dish with pheasant pieces and cover with stock. Cook in a moderate oven for 1 hour. Add port or red wine to the casserole and cook for a further 30 minutes. To thicken the stock, make a beurre-manié (refer glossary) and add to casserole, a little at a time and cook until slightly thickened. Before serving, sprinkle with chopped parsley. Serve with orange salad and french fries.

RABBIT IN CREAM SAUCE

1¾ litres game stock
1 rabbit
50 g butter
225 g lean bacon
100 g fat salt pork
½ teaspoon tarragon
1 teaspoon rosemary
1 teaspoon thyme
150 ml cognac
425 ml cream
50 g flour
50 g butter
salt and pepper

serves 4

Cut the rabbit into serving pieces and pat dry with a clean cloth. Cover the pieces of rabbit with seasoned flour. Heat a little butter in frying pan and sauté the rabbit until golden brown. Line an earthenware dish with alternate layers of thinly sliced lean bacon, fat salt pork, tarragon, rosemary and thyme. Place the rabbit pieces on top of the herb layer and pour cognac over. Place in a hot oven for 15 minutes, remove and set cognac alight. Cover casserole with stock and return to oven and cook for a further 20 minutes. Reduce heat to low. Make a beurre-manié (refer glossary) and add to the casserole in small quantities, stirring until thick. Add cream to casserole, mix thoroughly, cover and return to heat for 30 minutes. Do not allow to boil. Serve with scalloped potatoes, carrots in honey and fresh peas.

Wine: Red. Burgundy.
         White. Pouilly-fuissé.

RAGOUT OF RABBIT

1 rabbit or hare
6 rashers bacon
2 small onions
75 g butter
75 g flour
1¼ litres stock
juice of 1 lemon
1 bay leaf
1 teaspoon paprika
salt and pepper

serves 4

Prepare and joint the rabbit or hare. Wipe and cut into serving pieces. Chop the bacon roughly, peel and dice the onions. Melt the butter in a frying pan and sauté the rabbit. Drain and place in a pan. Fry the bacon and onion until brown and add to casserole. Stir the flour into the butter and cook for 1 minute, remove from heat and slowly stir in some of the stock. When smooth, add remainder of the stock, return pan to the heat and cook until slightly thickened. Stir in the lemon juice then pour stock over rabbit and vegetables. Add the bay leaf, paprika, salt and pepper to taste. Cover pan and slowly bring to the boil, reduce heat and simmer for 30 minutes. Remove lid and cook for a further 30 minutes. Serve immediately.

JUGGED HARE

1 hare
25 g dripping
2 rashers bacon
25 g flour
575 ml game stock
1 large onion, stuck with 6 cloves
1 carrot
1 teaspoon mixed herbs
½ teaspoon mace
1 bay leaf
6 whole peppercorns
275 ml red wine
100 ml port dregs
salt and pepper
25 g redcurrant jelly

serves 4

Bleed the hare and reserve blood (optional). Joint the hare, wipe with a damp cloth and fry the pieces in dripping until golden brown. Transfer hare to a pot. Chop the bacon and cook in the dripping. Blend the flour with a little of the stock and add both flour and remaining stock to the pan and stir until smooth. Pour stock over the hare. Add the whole onion stuck with cloves and sliced carrot, mixed herbs, mace, bay leaf and whole peppercorns. Cover and cook gently in a moderate oven or over a low flame on top of the stove for 3 hours. Bring back to the boil and add red wine and port dregs. Reduce heat to simmer again. If blood is being used, just before serving, remove the cloved onion and add blood and redcurrant jelly. Season to taste with salt and pepper. Do not allow to boil or the blood will clot. Serve immediately.

Wine: Red. Bordeaux.
         White. Pouilly-fumé.

TEAL WITH GREEN GRAPES

8 teal ducks
500 g cooked wild rice
1 pinch thyme
150 g honey
50 g butter
275 ml game stock
200 ml white wine
100 ml sherry
1 pinch cinnamon
75 g flour
50 ml lemon juice
25 g brown sugar
150 g seedless green grapes
25 g blanched almonds
25 g walnuts
salt and pepper

serves 4

Clean teals inside and out and rub skin with salt. Mix the wild rice, thyme, salt and pepper to taste and stuff each bird with a little of this mixture. Truss the birds and coat each one with honey. Heat the butter in a frying pan and gently sauté the teals until golden brown on all sides. Add white wine and sherry and cook for 20 minutes. Remove birds and place on a serving dish, keep warm in a low oven. Reduce the liquid by half by placing it in a saucepan and boiling rapidly with the lid off. Blend flour, lemon juice and sugar together and slowly pour into the reduced liquid, stirring until thickened. Pour this mixture over the teal, cover and turn heat up slightly and cook for 15 minutes. Add grapes and cook for a further 5 minutes. Remove birds from oven, sprinkle with ground almonds and walnuts and serve immediately.

Wine: Red. Margaux, Musigny or Beaujolais.

Roast Curried Lamb

ROAST CURRIED LAMB

2-kilo leg of lamb
1¼ litres red wine
3 cloves garlic
150 g curry powder (refer glossary)
25 mm piece ginger root
3 teaspoons chilli powder
2 teaspoons rosemary
2 teaspoons marjoram
100 ml oil

serves 6

Trim all the fat from the leg of lamb and reserve. Place the red wine in a large dish and crush the garlic cloves into the wine. Marinate the lamb in this mixture for 24 hours or longer if desired, turning the lamb at regular intervals to ensure that the meat is properly marinated. Mix the curry powder, grated ginger root and chilli powder with a little of the marinade mixture to form a thick paste. Using a spatula, spread the curry mixture over the leg of lamb (underside) then sprinkle over half the rosemary and marjoram. Place the lamb in a baking dish, curry side down and proceed coating the second side. Sprinkle the top with remaining rosemary and marjoram. Leave to stand for several hours. Place a little oil in the baking dish and place lamb in a moderate oven, allowing 20 minutes per ½-kilo plus 20 minutes extra cooking time (15 minutes for rare). Baste regularly. For the last 20 minutes of cooking, turn the oven up to high so the curry paste turns crisp and dark in colour. Place the meat on a pre-heated serving dish and keep in a warm oven. Make a gravy by using the pan drippings and curry scrapings, marinade juice and thicken with a little cornflour. Strain through a fine sieve and serve separately. To serve, remove the hard outer crust of curry paste and discard leaving the softer curry powder on top. Carve the lamb with the grain making sure that each slice has some of the curry on top. Serve with roast potatoes, carrots, parsnips and green peas.

Wine: Red. Hermitage, Cabernet Sauvignon or Margaux.

DRY LAMB CURRY

675 g shoulder lamb
575 ml stock
50 ml oil
5 tomatoes
265 ml coconut milk (refer note below)
150 g curry powder (refer glossary)

POUNDED INGREDIENTS
2 onions
4 cloves garlic
2 red chillies
1 green chilli
50 mm fresh ginger root

serves 6

Trim the fat from lamb and cut flesh into bite-sized pieces. Heat oil in a frying pan, add meat and fry until well sealed on all sides. Place in a saucepan with stock and bring to the boil. Cook for 45 minutes then strain through a sieve and reserve 225 ml of stock. Place all pounded ingredients in a mortar and pound with a pestle until a paste forms (or use a liquidiser). Place curry powder and pounded ingredients in a frying pan with 2 teaspoons oil and fry until fragrant or until a red oily film appears on top. To obtain the best flavour, fry very quickly over a high heat adding a little water to prevent burning. Place the lamb in a saucepan and add coconut milk. Simmer over a low heat for 15 minutes then add fried ingredients. Skin the tomatoes, chop roughly and add to lamb, season with salt and pepper and continue to cook until meat is tender and most of the juices have been absorbed. Serve the curry on a bed of plain boiled rice with sambals of tomato and onion in sour cream and cucumber in yoghurt.
NOTE: If coconut milk is unavailable, use 150 g dessicated coconut soaked in 500 ml boiling water. Knead the mixture and squeeze out several times. Strain and reserve milk.

LAMB STEW

675 g lamb
3 onions
4 potatoes
1 turnip
1 leek
2 carrots
1 stalk celery
1 pinch rosemary
1 pinch basil
100 g parsley
225 ml white wine
450 ml veal or chicken stock
25 g flour
salt and pepper

serves 6

Wipe and trim lamb and cut into small pieces. Peel and slice onions, potatoes and turnip. Wash and slice white part of leek, carrots and celery. Place the meat and vegetables in layers in a saucepan and sprinkle the top with rosemary, basil and parsley. In a separate saucepan bring the white wine and stock to the boil. Cook for several minutes then pour over the lamb. Cover saucepan and cook over a gentle heat for 1½ hours or until meat is tender. Blend the flour with a little cold water then stir into casserole to thicken. Keep over a low heat until ready for use. Serve with creamed potatoes and spinach or plain boiled rice.

Wine: Red. Beaujolais.
        Rosé d'Anjou.

ROAST CROWN OF LAMB

12 lamb loin ribs (in one piece)
50 g butter
25 ml olive oil
25 g thyme

STUFFING
450 g pork or veal forcemeat
2 onions
50 g parsley
1 teaspoon thyme
1 egg yolk
75 g breadcrumbs
salt and pepper

serves 4

Using a very sharp knife, trim the skin and fat from ribs to about 8 cm from the top of the bones. Clean each bone thoroughly so the ends stand up separately. Trim excess fat from inside the ribs and reserve. With skin side inwards, make a 'crown' — tying the two bone ends together securely with string. Make the stuffing by peeling and finely chopping the onion, fry gently for a few minutes in butter until soft but not brown. Combine forcemeat, onion, parsley, thyme and breadcrumbs together and bind with egg yolk. Season to taste with salt and pepper. Fill the hollow of the 'crown' with stuffing and place the reserved fat on top. Rub oil on the outside of the meat and rub in the thyme. Wrap the bone-ends in tinfoil to avoid burning and place the lamb in a baking dish with butter and oil. Roast in a moderate oven allowing 25 minutes per ½ kilo plus 25 minutes extra cooking time. (20 minutes plus 20 extra if desired rare.) Remove from pan and place on a warm serving dish. Remove tinfoil and replace with paper crowns. Serve with duchesse potatoes, sliced green beans and carrots in honey and sesame seeds.

Wine: Well-matured red. Saint-émilion, Côte de Beaune or Hermitage.

Beef Ragout

BEEF RAGOUT

1 kilo rump steak
1 large onion
2 carrots
2 stalks celery
1 leek
50 g butter or lard
25 ml oil
225 ml dry red wine
1 litre beef stock
2 teaspoons mustard powder
1 teaspoon marjoram
1 teaspoon oregano
50 g parsley
1 teaspoon vinegar
1 small cucumber
170 g mushrooms
salt and pepper

serves 6

Wipe the steak with a clean cloth, trim off fat and cut meat into bite-sized pieces. Peel and slice the onion, wash and slice carrots, celery and leek. Heat the butter or lard in a large frying pan and gently sauté the meat until sealed on all sides. Transfer meat to an enamel saucepan. Using the same frying pan, sauté the vegetables until soft but not brown, drain and add to saucepan with meat. Pour the red wine and beef stock over meat, bring to the boil then reduce heat and simmer for 1 hour. Blend the mustard powder with vinegar and a little of the hot stock. Place in a frying pan and stir until smooth over a gentle heat. Add marjoram, oregano and parsley and cook for 2 minutes. Add to beef. Peel and finely slice the cucumber, wipe, trim and slice the mushrooms. Fry gently in a little butter and when soft, add to beef ragout. Cook for a further 30 minutes or until meat is quite tender. Adjust seasoning and serve immediately.

BEEF CARBONNADE

900 g rump steak
50 g lard
1 onion
1 carrot
1 leek
225 g green beans
50 ml oil
375 ml can of lager or beer
50 g butter
50 g flour
500 ml beef stock
1 teaspoon sugar
1 teaspoon ginger powder
2 limes or lemons
salt and pepper

serves 6

Wipe the beef and trim off any excess fat. Cut meat into chunky pieces. Melt the lard and fry beef until well sealed on all sides. Transfer meat to a casserole dish and place in a warm oven. Peel and finely slice the onion, wash and slice carrot, leek and beans. Heat oil in a clean frying pan and sauté the vegetables, one at a time, until soft but not brown. Add vegetables to beef and cover with lager or beer. Cook in a moderate oven for 1 hour. Make a roux by melting the butter in a frying pan, stir in the flour and cook for 1 minute. Remove from heat and slowly add stock, stirring until smooth. Return to heat and add sugar, ginger powder and the juice of limes or lemons. Cook for 3 minutes then pour over the beef. Simmer for a further 45 minutes then serve with plain boiled rice.

Wine: Red. Bordeaux, Beajolais or Côtes du Rhône.

FILLET OF BEEF WITH LOBSTER

6 fillets of steak, 170 g each
1 small lobster tail
12 artichoke bottoms
1 pinch oregano
25 ml oil
275 ml madeira sauce (refer page 115)

serves 6

Wipe the pieces of steak and trim off any excess fat. Place meat on a flat surface and cut a hole in the centre of each piece without going right through to the bottom. Remove meat 'cap' and reserve. Place the steaks, hole side down on a grilling plate, brush with a little oil, sprinkle with oregano and grill for 3-4 minutes. Remove from grill and turn hole side up. Chop the lobster tail into 6 equal parts and place 1 portion in the hole of each piece of steak. Place reserved 'caps' on top of lobster, brush with a little oil then place under the grill and cook for a further 4-5 minutes, depending on how rare or well done the meat is required. Allow 5 minutes each side for medium and 7-8 minutes for well done. Remove meat from grill and place 2 artichoke bottoms on each plate. Put the steak on top of the artichokes and serve immediately with madeira sauce.

STEAK PARCELS

6 fillets of steak, 170 g each
1 can oysters, 200 g
2 teaspoons worcestershire sauce
25 g parsley
1 dash tabasco
2 teaspoons oregano
450 g shortcrust pastry (refer page 113)
egg white for sealing
oil for deep frying

serves 6

Rub the steaks with salt and freshly ground black pepper. Mix together the oysters, worcestershire sauce, parsley, tabasco and oregano, mash well. Roll out the pastry to 3 mm thickness and cut out 6 circles, using a bread and butter plate as a guide. Coat each steak with the oyster mixture and place in the centre of the pastry circle. Coat the pastry edges with a little egg white and bring into the centre to form small parcels. Press the edges together firmly to seal. Prick the pastry in several places to allow air to escape. Heat the oil in a deep pan and when hot, gently lower the steak parcels into the pan and cook for approximately 6 minutes or until pastry is golden brown. If steak is preferred medium or well done, it can be grilled for a few minutes first, then set aside to cool down before proceeding with the recipe. Serve with grilled tomatoes, sautéed mushrooms and french fries.

Wine: Red. Margaux, Bordeaux or Hermitage.

SAVOURY MEAT LOAF

450 g lean minced rump steak
1 large onion
2 cloves garlic
50 g chopped parsley
1 teaspoon basil
1 teaspoon marjoram
1 teaspoon paprika
1 teaspoon chilli powder
50 g tomato purée
50 g fresh breadcrumbs
1 egg yolk, beaten
75 g flour
salt and pepper

serves 4

Place the minced beef in a mixing bowl. Peel and grate the onion, crush the garlic and add to beef. Mix in the parsley, basil, marjoram, paprika, chilli powder and tomato purée. When well blended mix in the breadcrumbs, beaten egg yolk and sifted flour. If mixture is too dry add a small quantity of stock or tomato sauce. Put the meat mixture into a boiler, pat down well to make sure all the air has been extracted, cover with greaseproof paper and tie lid in place. Stand the boiler in a shallow baking dish with approximately 25 mm water. Bring to the boil over a rapid heat then transfer to a pre-heated moderate oven and cook for 1½ hours, topping up water level if necessary. Remove from pan, drain off excess fat and juice and reserve. Turn meat out onto a flat plate and keep warm. Return pan juices to saucepan and boil down until quantity is reduced by two-thirds. Pour liquid over meat loaf and serve hot with chilli sauce or spicy tomato sauce. This dish can also be served cold.

Wine: Light-bodied red. Claret, Chinon or Beaujolais.

Beef Curry

BEEF CURRY

1 kilo rump steak

75 mm ginger root

2 large onions

3 cloves garlic

100 g chilli powder

150 g curry powder (refer glossary)

575 ml beef stock

450 ml coconut milk (refer dry lamb curry, page 81)

150 ml lime or lemon juice

salt and pepper

oil for frying

serves 6-8

Wipe beef and trim off excess fat. Cut into bite-sized pieces. Grate together the ginger and onions, crush garlic and place in a frying pan with a little oil. Fry for several minutes then stir in the chilli powder. Cook for 2 minutes then add curry powder blended with a little coconut milk to form a paste. Fry until a red oily film appears on top. Add the meat and stir for 5 minutes. Place the meat and onion mixture into a large saucepan, add beef stock and cook over a gentle heat for 30 minutes. Add half the coconut milk and cook for a further 15 minutes before adding the remaining coconut milk. Cook for a further 15 minutes then add lime or lemon juice, salt and pepper to taste. Simmer gently for 30 minutes, stirring from time to time to prevent sticking. Serve with sambals of grated hard-boiled egg whites and yolks, finely chopped shallots, onion, fried garlic, raisins, coconut, bananas, cucumber and tomatoes. Serve with plain boiled rice and hot mango chutney.

SHREDDED BEEF WITH GINGER

500 g fillet of beef

50 mm ginger root

½ onion, grated

2 cloves garlic, crushed

50 ml sherry

25 ml soya sauce

50 ml sesame or peanut oil

25 g cornflour

2 teaspoons chilli powder

25 g butter

25 ml oil for frying

serves 6

Wipe beef with a damp cloth and slice very thinly. Cut slices into narrow strips. Peel the ginger root and cut into thin slices. Combine beef, ginger, grated onion, crushed garlic, sherry, soya sauce, oil, cornflour and chilli. Mix thoroughly so that the beef is well coated. Refrigerate for several hours to marinate. This mixture can stand in the refrigerator for 2-3 days before using. Melt the butter in a frying pan and add the oil. When hot, add the beef mixture and 'stir-fry' over a high heat for 5 minutes. Fry a little longer if beef is preferred well done. Serve immediately with bean sprouts or rice.

Wine: Red. Beaujolais or Claret.
          Rosé. Mateus or d'Anjou.

BRAISED VEAL

4 veal escalopes or chops
1 onion
1 clove garlic
1 carrot
100 g mushrooms
225 ml dry white wine
500 ml veal stock
2 teaspoons mixed herbs
5 dashes worcestershire sauce
25 g cornflour
salt and pepper
oil for frying

serves 4

Place the trimmed veal in a pan with a little oil or butter. Seal on all sides, drain and place in a shallow casserole dish. Peel and slice the onion, crush garlic and brown in the same frying pan as the meat was cooked in. Scrape and slice carrot, peel, trim and slice mushrooms and add to pan with onion and garlic. Cook for 1-2 minutes and add to casserole. Pour the veal stock into a saucepan and bring to the boil, add mixed herbs and worcestershire sauce, cook for 2 minutes then reduce heat to simmer. Add the white wine and remove from heat. Blend the cornflour with a little cold water and stir into the stock. Return to heat and stir until slightly thickened. Adjust seasoning, pour stock over meat and vegetables, cover and cook in a moderate oven for 1 hour. Reduce heat to simmer and cook for a further 30 minutes. Serve with scalloped potatoes and green beans.

ROAST FILLET OF VEAL

2 veal fillets
50 g mixed herbs
lard or dripping

MARINADE
3 cloves garlic
225 ml veal stock
2 red chillies
1 carrot
1 stalk celery
1 onion
1 pinch mixed herbs
100 ml oil
175 ml white wine
salt and pepper

GRAVY
200 ml marinade mixture
75 ml pan drippings
25 ml milk
50 g flour

serves 6

Crush the garlic into a saucepan, add veal stock and slowly bring to the boil, reduce heat and simmer for 10 minutes. Chop the chillies finely, slice the carrot, celery and onion and add to stock together with mixed herbs. Cook for 2 minutes, remove from heat and allow to cool completely. When cold stir in the olive oil and white wine. Season to taste with salt and pepper. Trim the veal fillets and wipe with a damp cloth. Place the meat in an oblong earthenware dish and pour the marinade over. Set aside for several hours, turning meat at regular intervals to ensure all meat is evenly coated. Strain the marinade into a bowl and reserve 200 ml for gravy. Pat the fillets dry and coat with the mixed herbs. Place them in a roasting dish with lard or dripping and bake in a moderate oven for 30-45 minutes. Remove meat and place on a warm serving dish in a low oven. To make gravy, place marinade mixture and pan drippings into a saucepan and re-heat. Blend the flour with a little of the milk and stir into the gravy. When smooth bring to the boil and cook for 2 minutes. Season to taste with salt and pepper, reduce heat and add remaining milk. Do not boil. Serve separately in a warmed gravy boat.

Wine: Red. Malbec or Sauvignon.

VEAL WELLINGTON

2 veal fillets
50 g lard
350 g oysters, tinned
2 teaspoons worcestershire sauce
1 teaspoon mixed herbs
10 rashers streaky bacon
450 g ruff puff pastry (refer page 112)
1 egg white
salt and white pepper

serves 4

Wipe the veal fillets with a clean cloth, place in a roasting dish with lard and bake in a moderate oven for 30-45 minutes. Place oysters, worcestershire sauce and mixed herbs in a bowl and mash well. Add salt and pepper to taste. Roll out pastry to 3 mm thickness and cut two oblong strips, wide enough to roll around the fillets. Remove veal from oven and pat dry. Allow to cool slightly. Spread the oyster mixture on the bacon rashers and place cross-wise on the pastry. Place the veal fillets on the oysters and bring bacon strips up over the top of the meat. Brush a little egg white along the pastry edges and bring ends up to meet in the centre. Press together firmly to seal then turn the roll over. Seal the ends and trim with a pastry cutter. Cut patterns from the left-over pastry, brush egg white over the top of the veal wellington and secure the decorations. Place on a baking tray and bake in a moderate oven for 45 minutes or until pastry is golden brown. Serve immediately.

Wine: Red. Hermitage, Côte de Nuits or Fleurie.

VEAL CASSEROLE

675 g lean veal
25 g lard
1 onion
2 cloves garlic
1 teaspoon veal seasoning or
  mixed herbs
50 g chopped chives
50 g chopped parsley
1 teaspoon red chillies, chopped
25 mm piece ginger root, grated
2 teaspoons mustard powder
700 ml veal stock
75 g flour
salt and pepper

serves 4-6

Wipe veal with a clean cloth and trim off any excess fat. Cut into bite-sized pieces. Sift the flour, salt and pepper together and roll veal pieces in this mixture, coating well on all sides. Melt the lard in a frying pan and when hot, quickly brown the meat on all sides. Remove from pan, drain and place in a casserole dish. Peel and finely chop the onion, crush garlic and fry in the same pan. Add veal seasoning or mixed herbs, chives, parsley, chopped chillies and grated ginger and cook for 2 minutes. Add this mixture to veal casserole. Place the mustard powder in frying pan and blend with a little stock. Bring to the boil and slowly add the remaining stock. Boil until liquid is reduced by half then pour over the veal. Adjust seasoning, cover and cook in a slow oven for 1½ hours. Serve with baked onions, creamed potato and spinach.

Wine: Red. Cabernet, Malbec or Sauvignon.

Veal Casserole

SPAGHETTI WITH VEAL SAUCE

450 g lean minced veal
25 g butter
1 onion, diced
3 large cloves garlic
1 litre beef stock
1 bay leaf
6 black peppercorns
juice and peel of 1 lemon
2 tomatoes
75 g tomato purée
1 teaspoon basil
1 teaspoon oregano
25 g parsley
salt and pepper
450 g spaghetti

serves 4

Place the minced veal in a frying pan without oil or butter and 'dry fry', stirring to separate the meat and making sure all pieces are nicely browned. Transfer veal to a large saucepan. Melt the butter in a frying pan and sauté the diced onion and crushed cloves of garlic. When brown, add to veal and pour beef stock over. Add the bay leaf, whole peppercorns and juice and peel of lemon. Cook for 15 minutes then reduce heat to simmer and cook for a further 30 minutes. Crack the skins of tomatoes by pouring boiling water over, remove skins and finely chop the flesh. Add flesh and tomato purée to meat together with basil, oregano, parsley, salt and pepper. Cook, stirring occassionally for 1 hour or until most of the liquid has been absorbed. It may be necessary to turn the heat up slightly during the last 5 minutes of cooking. Remove bay leaf and lemon peel. Pour the meat sauce over spaghetti, sprinkle with parmesan cheese and serve immediately.

VEAL KOFTAS

550 g lean minced veal
2 onions, diced
3 cloves garlic
1 pinch sage
1 pinch basil
1 teaspoon cayenne pepper
4 shallots, diced
1 teaspoon tomato purée
1 teaspoon cinnamon
25 g flour
2 egg yolks
salt and pepper
oil for frying

SAUCE
300 ml brown stock
25 g flour
25 g butter
1 teaspoon turmeric
50 g curry powder (refer glossary)
4 dashes tabasco
salt and pepper

serves 6

Peel and finely dice the onions and garlic and sauté in oil until soft. Place minced veal in a bowl and add the onions and garlic, sage, basil, cayenne pepper and diced shallots. Mix with a fork until well blended. Stir in the tomato purée and sift in the cinnamon and flour. Make a well in the centre and add egg yolks. Beat the mixture with a fork and add salt and pepper to taste. Add more flour to bind if necessary. Using slightly moistened hands, form the mixture into small balls about the size of a walnut. Place in hot oil, a few at a time, and deep fry until meat is golden brown. Drain and place on a warm serving dish in a low oven. To make sauce heat stock slowly and keep it just off the boil. Blend the flour, butter, turmeric and curry powder together and when smooth, drop teaspoonfuls into the stock, stirring to prevent lumps. When sauce has thickened season to taste with tabasco, salt and pepper. Cook for 10 minutes then pour sauce over meat balls. Serve immediately.

Wine: Red. Malbec or Sauvignon.
         Rosé. Mateus or d'Anjou.

PORK WITH COCONUT

500 g lean pork
3 teaspoons coriander pods
2 teaspoons chillies
½ teaspoon tarragon
1 teaspoon cinnamon
2 teaspoons paprika
2 teaspoons cayenne pepper
2 teaspoons garlic salt
1 teaspoon black pepper
50 g sesame seeds
170 g dessicated coconut
boiling water to cover
575 ml veal stock
25 g cornflour
oil for frying

serves 4

Wipe pork with a damp cloth and cut into 25 mm pieces. Combine the crushed coriander, chillies, tarragon, cinnamon, paprika, cayenne, garlic salt, black pepper and sesame seeds and stir thoroughly. Coat the pork pieces with this mixture and allow to stand for 15 minutes. Place the dessicated coconut in a bowl and pour boiling water over to moisten. Heat stock and add coconut. Allow to simmer gently. Heat oil in a frying pan and sauté the pork until fragrant and sealed on all sides. Place the pork and pan drippings into the stock and cook over a gentle heat for 1 hour or until pork is thoroughly cooked. Blend cornflour with a little cold water and add to pork. Adjust seasoning and stir until the mixture is slightly thickened. Serve immediately with butter rice or fried rice.

SPICED PORK WITH PEPPERS

450 g lean pork
2 green capsicums
2 green chillies
oil for frying

MARINADE
225 ml soya sauce
100 ml honey
1 onion, grated
3 cloves garlic
2 teaspoons ginger powder
1 teaspoon chilli powder
1 teaspoon cayenne pepper

SAUCE
200 ml marinade mixture
25 g cornflour
50 ml red wine
salt and pepper

serves 4

Trim any surplus fat from meat and wipe pork with a damp cloth. Slice very thinly and cut into 'julienne' strips, approximately 3 mm wide. Wash the capsicums and chillies and cut into dice. Place the soya sauce and honey in a saucepan and heat through gently. When well blended remove from heat and transfer to an earthenware bowl. Peel and grate the onion, crush garlic and add to bowl together with remaining marinade ingredients. Place the pork in the marinade and refrigerate overnight. Remove the meat and drain on kitchen paper. Heat oil in a frying pan and cook pork over a high heat for a few minutes to seal on all sides. Drain and transfer to a serving dish in a warm oven. Fry the capsicums and chillies in a little oil for a few minutes or until peppers become slightly brown but not soft. Drain and add to pork. Strain the marinade mixture into a saucepan and bring to the boil, reduce heat and simmer. If honey starts to burn, reduce heat to very low or place an asbestos mat under the saucepan. Blend together the cornflour and red wine. When smooth, stir into the marinade mixture. Adjust seasoning then pour sauce over pork and peppers and serve immediately.

Wine: White. Pinot Blanc or Traminer.
         Red. Saint-émilion or Chambertin.

B.B.Q. SPARE RIBS

1½ kilos pork spare ribs

MARINADE:
200 g honey
75 ml vinegar
200 ml soya sauce
250 ml red wine
75 g brown sugar
3 cloves garlic, crushed
25 ml lemon juice
25 g ginger powder
25 ml sherry
2 teaspoons marjoram
2 teaspoons rosemary
2 teaspoons sage
1 teaspoon cayenne pepper

serves 4

Mix together all dry ingredients, add honey and soya sauce and blend thoroughly. Stir in red wine, lemon juice and sherry. Wipe the spare ribs and trim off any excess fat. Cut into 8 cm lengths and marinate in an earthenware bowl for 1 or 2 days. The longer the bones marinate, the more tasty. They can marinate in this mixture for 5 days before cooking. When ready for use, dry the spare ribs and either barbeque over live coals, grill under a hot grill or bake in a moderate oven for 1 hour. Do not allow them to become too dry. If necessary coat with olive oil and red wine in equal parts to keep moist. Serve with hot chilli sauce or spicy tomato sauce and green salad.

Wine: Red. Saint-émilion, Hermitage or Beaujolais.
Rosé d'Anjou
White. Graves or Riesling.

PORK CHOPS WITH CUCUMBER SAUCE

12 lean pork loin chops
575 ml vegetable stock
1 large onion
1 clove garlic
3 large cucumbers
1 pinch nutmeg
salt and pepper

MARINADE
300 ml red wine
100 ml peanut oil
1 onion, grated
1 teaspoon mace

serves 6

Combine all the marinade ingredients and beat until smooth. Wipe the chops with a damp cloth and place them in an earthenware bowl. Pour the marinade over the top and set aside for several hours. When ready for use, remove and pat dry. Place chops under a hot grill and seal on both sides. Reduce heat and continue to grill until chops are well cooked and tender, approximately 30 minutes. Place the stock in a saucepan and bring to the boil. Peel and finely dice the onion, add to stock and boil for 15 minutes. Remove from heat. Peel and crush garlic, peel and finely chop cucumbers. Place stock, onion, garlic and cucumbers in a liquidiser and blend for 30 seconds. The cucumber should not be completely smooth. Return to saucepan, re-heat and season to taste with salt, pepper and sprinkle with nutmeg. Pour sauce over chops or serve separately in a gravy-boat.

Wine: Red. Beaujolais, Chambertin or Cabernet Hermitage.
Rosé. Mateus.
White. Chablis or Pouilly-fuissé.

Pork Chops with Cucumber Sauce

SWEET AND SOUR PORK

1 kilo pork fillets

cornflour

oil for frying

1 leek, sliced

1 onion, peeled and diced

1 carrot, sliced

1 stalk celery, sliced

2 red chillies, sliced

1 green capsicum, diced

MARINADE

25 ml honey

50 ml soya sauce

25 ml dry white wine

25 ml sherry or port

2 teaspoons ginger root, shredded

8 spring onions, chopped

SAUCE

100 ml wine vinegar

75 g brown sugar

225 ml pineapple juice

25 g cornflour or arrowroot

salt and pepper to taste

serves 6

Trim the pork fillets and wipe with a damp cloth. Cut into bite-sized pieces. Make the marinade by beating together the honey, soya sauce, wine and sherry or port. Mix in the ginger root and spring onions. Place the meat in marinade mixture and leave to stand for several hours or overnight if possible, making sure that all pieces are well covered. Remove meat and roll in cornflour. Heat the oil and fry the meat until it is nicely browned on all sides, drain and keep warm on the side of the stove or in the oven. In a separate frying pan, 'stir-fry' the vegetables, shaking pan frequently to prevent sticking, until they are soft. Drain and reserve. Make the sauce by heating the vinegar in a saucepan, add sugar and stir whilst bringing to the boil. Allow to boil until sugar has dissolved. Reduce heat to simmer and add the pineapple juice. Blend the cornflour with a little cold water and stir into the sauce. Cook, stirring, for 2 minutes. Pour sauce over the vegetables and keep warm in the oven. Remove the pork pieces, roll in cornflour once more and re-fry for 1 minute. Drain and place meat on a large serving dish. Pour the sauce and vegetable mixture over the top and serve immediately with plain boiled rice.

B.B.Q. PORK FILLETS

2 pork fillets

MARINADE

100 ml golden syrup

25 g ginger root, shredded

1 large onion, grated

3 cloves garlic, crushed

500 ml soya sauce

100 ml dry sherry

100 ml peanut oil

25 ml white vinegar

1 bay leaf

25 ml lemon juice

salt and pepper to taste

serves 6

Wipe pork fillet with a damp cloth and cut into bite-sized pieces. Combine all the marinade ingredients together and beat with a wire whisk until well blended. Place the pork in the marinade, making sure all pieces are well covered and place in the refrigerator for several hours or overnight if possible. Remove from marinade when ready for use, pat dry with kitchen paper and barbeque over live coals or grill under a medium heat for 30 minutes. Transfer to a baking dish and place in a moderate oven and continue to cook for a further 20 minutes or until pork is thoroughly cooked. Serve with apple sauce, gravy or thickened marinade and grilled pineapple rings.

Wine: Red. Beaujolais or Chambertin.
White. Anjou or Graves.

BUTTER RICE

100 g butter
225 g long grain rice
chicken stock to cover
salt and pepper

serves 4

Melt the butter in a heavy-based frying pan and add the raw rice grains. Cook over a high heat, stirring continuously to prevent burning, until rice is a rich golden brown colour. Remove from heat. Place rice in a saucepan and cover with chicken stock, approximately 25 mm above rice level. Bring to the boil and boil rapidly for 5 minutes. Reduce heat until stock is only just on the boil and cook rice until all the liquid is absorbed. Do not stir the rice during cooking. Season to taste with salt and pepper and serve immediately.

FRIED RICE

250 g rice, cooked
75 g streaky bacon or ham
½ onion, grated
100 g prawns
50 g parsley
2 eggs
salt and pepper
butter and oil for frying
10 spring onions, chopped

serves 6

Finely chop the bacon or ham and place in a wok or frying pan. Sauté until crisp and golden and all the fat has melted. If using ham, fry in a little butter until golden. Add the grated onion and cook until tender. Add prawns and parsley, cook for 3 minutes then remove from pan and reserve. Beat the eggs until smooth. Using the same wok or frying pan, cook the eggs 'omelet style'. When cooked, remove from heat and cut into small pieces. Add to bacon and onion. Season the pre-cooked rice with salt and pepper. Heat butter and oil in the wok and add rice. Stir over a high heat for several minutes or until the butter has been absorbed. Add the reserved bacon or ham, onion, prawns, parsley and egg. Heat through thoroughly. Just before serving, stir in the chopped spring onions.

Optional additives: Cooked peas, water chestnuts, pork, chicken, corn kernels and garlic.

NOTE: If you do not have a wok, use a light-based frying pan or a shallow baking dish.

Desserts & Pastry

Some people have a sweet tooth, some don't and others are on a diet! Therefore it is wise to know your guests' tastes in advance so that an appropriate dessert can be made to suit all palates.

The dessert should also complement the preceding courses. If a light entrée and an elaborate main course are served, a light dessert is more appropriate than a heavy one. However, if a substantial entrée and lighter main course are served or, in the case of a two-course meal, the heavier baked desserts may be served with equal satisfaction. The climate or time of the year should also be taken into account when planning the menu as very few people have the desire to eat ice-cream or other frozen desserts when it's snowing outside and, like-wise, to eat heavy baked desserts in tropical areas or in the height of summer.

The cheeseboard is something which can be offered in lieu of a dessert and is becoming a very popular course of the meal. There are no 'written laws' as to which way about cheese should be served; in a French or continental home you would expect cheese before a dessert whereas in a colonial or western home, cheese would be presented after the dessert, in which case it would be followed by coffee and port or liqueurs. Petits Fours — a name adopted for many kinds of small fancy cakes or chocolates can also be served with coffee. If a sumptuous dinner is being served, many connoisseurs maintain that cheese is out of place, so it is up to the hostess to decide whether it is a necessary part of the meal or not.

Guests should also be given the choice of wine, port or liqueurs with their dessert, cheese and coffee.

BRANDY PAVLOVA

4 egg whites
225 g castor sugar
50 g cinnamon powder
1 teaspoon cornflour
2 teaspoons brandy
1 teaspoon vinegar
575 ml cream
1 punnet strawberries

serves 6

Using eggs at room temperature, separate the yolks from the whites and place the whites in a lukewarm bowl. Whisk until stiff peaks form then slowly add the castor sugar, a teaspoonful at a time, and continue to whisk or beat at high speed until sugar has been used up and is nearly dissolved. The mixture should be beaten for at least 5 minutes. Sift together the cinnamon and cornflour and mix into the beaten egg whites with a wooden spoon. Fold in the brandy and vinegar then turn mixture out onto a baking tray lined with greaseproof paper or aluminium foil. Use a spatula or flat knife to shape the mixture into a circle or square, making sure the top and sides are pressed down thoroughly to expel air. If desired, a piping bag can be used to make a 'hollow' pavlova. Place the baking tray in a warm oven for 15 minutes then reduce heat to low and bake for 2 hours. Turn oven off and allow the pavlova to cool down in the oven. When cool, turn the pavlova upside-down onto a flat serving plate and peel away the paper or foil. If the dessert is successful, the centre should drop to approximately 25 mm below the meringue exterior. Whip the cream and cover the top of the pavlova. Decorate with strawberries or other fruit such as Chinese gooseberries (Kiwi fruit), pineapple or passionfruit. The pavlova should be whitish-cream in colour, meringue on the outside and marshmallow in the middle. To test if pavlova is cooked, place a skewer through the middle and if it comes out dry, the dish is cooked.

NOTE: The whipping process of this dish is most important and will mean the success or otherwise of the pavlova. If sugar is added too quickly or the mixture is not beaten long enough to dissolve the sugar, it will result in a sticky mixture with caramel spots on the exterior.

GRANNY'S APPLE PIE

675 g 'granny smith' apples
½ lemon
50 g castor sugar
50 g demarara sugar
25 g flour
½ teaspoon nutmeg
½ teaspoon cinnamon sugar
25 g chopped raisins
25 g chopped sultanas
grated peel of ½ orange
grated peel of ½ lemon
50 ml orange juice
50 g butter
400 g shortcrust pastry

serves 4

Prepare the shortcrust pastry (refer page 113) adding in 2 teaspoons of cinnamon with the flour. Peel, core and slice the apples. Squeeze juice from half a lemon and sprinkle over the apples. Add a few spoonfuls of water and allow apples to soak for 30 minutes. Line a 22 cm pie plate with the pastry. Combine sugar, demarara sugar, flour, nutmeg and cinnamon sugar and sprinkle a little of this mixture over the pastry case. Add a layer of apple, raisins, sultanas, grated orange and lemon peel. Continue working in alternate layers until all ingredients have been used up. Add 50 ml of orange juice and dot with butter. Out of the remaining pastry, cut a pie lid, brush the edges with egg white and secure the lid in place. Make several holes in the pastry to allow air to escape. If desired, patterns can be cut out of left-over pastry and secured to the lid with egg white. Bake in a hot oven for 35-40 minutes or until pastry turns golden brown. Serve with freshly whipped cream.

PEAR FRITTERS

6 pears
575 ml brandy
12 cloves
fat for deep-frying
sugar
400 g sweet shortcrust pastry
  (refer page 113)

serves 6

Peel the pears, cut in half length-wise and remove centre cores. Place in an earthenware bowl and cover with brandy. Add cloves and allow to marinate for at least 7 days but preferably 14 days. When well marinated, drain pears and discard brandy and cloves. Roll out pastry to 3 mm thickness and cut 24 rounds about 25 mm wider than the pears. Place half a pear, flat side down on each of 12 rounds of pastry. Dampen edges with a little milk or egg white and place the remaining pastry rounds on top to form a lid. Seal edges tightly so they will not come apart during cooking. Heat oil in a large frying pan and deep fry the pears, two at a time, for 3 minutes or until pastry is golden brown. If fresh pears are not quite ripe, they should be simmered in a little of the brandy for a few minutes first. Drain the pear fritters and sprinkle with sugar. Serve with whipped cream.

WINE TRIFLE

1 stale swiss roll
1½ litres custard
1¼ litres fresh cream
170 ml port
170 ml dry sherry
170 g walnuts

serves 6-8

Slice the swiss roll and line the bottom and sides of a glass dessert bowl. Mix the port and sherry together and pour half over the cake. Allow to settle in then pour remaining liquid over. There should be a small amount of liquid on the top. If cake is not moist enough add more port and sherry in equal quantities. Make an egg custard and pour on top of the cake, making sure it is well covered. Leave to stand until cool. Whip the cream until stiff peaks form. Spread over the custard lightly with a spatula. Chop the walnuts and sprinkle on top. Refrigerate until ready for use. If preferred, brandy may be whipped into the cream.

FRUIT FONDUE

1 punnet strawberries
1 fresh pineapple
225 g seedless grapes
½ honeydew or cantaloupe melon
575 ml cream
225 g castor sugar
rum
kirsch
brandy

serves 6

Cut stalks from strawberries and wash thoroughly. Drain on kitchen paper. Cut pineapple in half and carefully cut out the fruit. Remove the core and cut into bite-sized pieces. Reserve the pineapple shell. Remove grapes from stalks, wash and drain. Using a melon baller, remove flesh from melon. Combine all the fruit in a large bowl and marinate in kirsch for several hours. In each half pineapple, place a flameproof dish filled with methylated spirits. Place strained fruit in separate dishes in the centre of the table. In front of each guest, place individual bowls of rum, kirsch, brandy, castor sugar and cream. Set a pineapple half at each end of the table, light the methylated spirits. Each guest selects a piece of fruit, dips it into one of the liquors to moisten, then into sugar. The fruit is then held over the flame until the sugar caramelises. The fruit is then dipped in cream and placed on a plate to cool before eating.

NOTE: If methylated spirit burns dry DO NOT pour more spirit into the same bowl. Remove the bowl with a cloth and replace it with a fresh bowl.

Fruit Fondue

RHUBARB CRUMBLE

800 g cooked rhubarb
25 ml lemon juice
1 teaspoon vanilla essence
225 g sugar
225 g self-raising flour
1 teaspoon cinnamon
100 g butter

serves 4-6

Strain the cooked rhubarb (reserving juice) and place in a casserole dish. Place the juice, lemon juice and vanilla in a saucepan and cook over a gentle heat for 3 minutes. Pour this mixture over the rhubarb. Sift the flour, sugar and cinnamon into a bowl and rub in the butter until mixture resembles fine breadcrumbs. Sprinkle on top of the rhubarb and bake in a moderate oven for 35 minutes. Serve with egg custard and cream.

COCONUT PUDDING

225 g sultanas
75 g sugar
225 g dessicated coconut
225 ml milk
75 g soft breadcrumbs
1 egg
50 g butter

serves 4-6

Wash the sultanas thoroughly under cold running water, drain and remove stalks. Pat dry on a clean cloth then place in a mixing bowl. Add sugar and coconut and mix well. Pour in the milk and add breadcrumbs. Beat the egg until smooth then pour into the fruit mixture. Grease a pie dish with butter and fill with coconut pudding. Bake in a moderate oven for 35 minutes. Serve immediately.

BREAD AND BUTTER CUSTARD

4 slices stale bread
50 g butter
25 g sultanas
25 g currants
2 eggs
75 g sugar
3 drops vanilla essence
575 ml milk
2 teaspoons nutmeg

serves 4

Butter the slices of bread and place in the bottom of a pie dish. Wash the sultanas and raisins thoroughly, dry and remove stalks. Place the fruit on top of the bread. Beat eggs together and add sugar. Stir in the vanilla and slowly pour in the milk, stirring continuously. When mixed sufficiently, pour the mixture into the pie dish and allow to stand for 30 minutes. Sprinkle top with grated or powdered nutmeg and bake in a moderate oven for 35 minutes or until nicely browned and set.

ORANGE AND PASSIONFRUIT CHEESECAKE

CRUST
225 g 'marie' biscuits
50 g cocoa powder
25 g sugar
170 ml margarine, melted

FILLING
2 eggs, separated
150 g sugar
50 g gelatine
1 can carnation milk, 400 ml
25 g grated orange peel
1 teaspoon vanilla essence
225 g philadelphia cheese
50 ml orange juice
50 g passionfruit

GLAZE
50 g sugar
25 g cornflour
50 ml orange juice
50 g passionfruit
25 g lemon juice

serves 8

To make the crust: Crush the biscuits with a rolling pin until they resemble fine breadcrumbs. Add sifted cocoa, sugar and melted margarine. Mix thoroughly and evenly then press the crust into the sides and bottom of a 22 cm spring-form cake tin and place in refrigerator to chill. To make the filling: Beat together the egg yolks, sugar and gelatine, stir in two-thirds of the carnation milk. Place remaining carnation milk in an ice tray in the freezer compartment until ice crystals form around the edges of the tray. Place the gelatine mixture in a saucepan over a gentle heat and stir until the gelatine dissolves and the mixture coats the back of a wooden spoon. Add orange peel and vanilla essence. Remove from heat and allow to cool. When cold, place in an electric mixer and blend in the philadelphia cheese. Chill the mixture until it moulds from the spoon. Beat the egg whites until peaks form. In a separate bowl, whip the reserved carnation milk until thick then add orange juice, passionfruit and gelatine mixture. Fold in the egg whites then pour the filling into the prepared biscuit case and chill for 7-8 hours or overnight. To make the glaze: Combine sugar and cornflour together. Mix in the orange juice and passionfruit, a little at a time, until smooth. Add lemon juice and stir over a low heat until sugar dissolves. Increase the heat slightly and allow the glaze to boil for a few minutes. Remove from heat and cool slightly. Spoon the glaze over the cheesecake and decorate top with slices of orange and passionfruit. Refrigerate until ready for use.

CHOCMINT CREAM

200 g light chocolate block
200 g dark chocolate block
150 ml green crème de menthe
150 ml clear crème de menthe
150 ml curaçao
2 egg yolks
1½ litres cream
3 drops peppermint essence

serves 6

Using a double boiler, fill the lower saucepan with water, bring to the boil then reduce heat so it is just off the boil. Break the chocolate into small pieces and place in the top of the double boiler, place over the hot water and stir until chocolate is melted. Stir in the green and clear crème de menthe and curaçao, a little at a time, stirring continuously. When well blended, remove from heat. Whisk the egg yolks and stir into the chocolate. Return to heat and simmer for a further 2 minutes. Remove from heat and allow to cool slightly. Whip the cream until quite firm. Reserve half the cream. When chocolate mixture has cooled sufficiently, fold in half the cream and fill parfait glasses to within 25 mm of the top. Stir the peppermint essence into the remaining cream. Place 3 teaspoons of green crème de menthe and a teaspoon of curaçao on top of each portion then spoon or pipe the cream to form peaks on top. Serve immediately.

FROZEN CHRISTMAS PUDDING

275 g vanilla ice cream
275 g chocolate ice cream
225 g mixed dried fruit
  (sultanas, currants, raisins)
225 g glacé cherries, red and
  green
225 g mixed chopped nuts
  (almonds, walnuts, hazels and
  brazils)
brandy
rum
150 ml cream
25 g coffee powder

serves 8

Mix together the 2 ice creams and place in freezer until ready for use. Combine the mixed fruit, cherries and nuts and cover with 2 parts of brandy to 1 part of rum. Seal the container and leave to marinate for at least 2 weeks but longer if possible. This mixture can stand for at least 2 months for best results. Strain alcohol and drain the fruit and nuts on kitchen paper. Remove ice cream from freezer and beat in the cream and coffee powder. Add fruit and nuts, making sure all are evenly distributed throughout the ice cream. Re-freeze until ready for use. If desired, a jelly mould can be used and the bottom decorated with whole nuts and angelica before adding ice cream. Serve with sweet wafer biscuits or meringue fingers.

NOTE: If fruit and nuts are not thoroughly dried before adding to ice cream, the mixture will not set properly.

Chocmint Cream/Frozen Christmas Pudding

CHRISTMAS PUDDING

300 g raisins
170 g sultanas
170 g currants
75 g glacé cherries, red and
  green
75 g mixed peel
150 g flour
225 g beef suet, minced
225 g demarara sugar
pinch salt
4 eggs
½ nutmeg, grated
50 g almonds, chopped
25 g walnuts, chopped
150 ml brandy
75 ml rum

serves 8

Wash the raisins, sultanas and currants thoroughly in cold water, strain and place in a clean cloth and pat dry. Remove stalks. Chop the cherries and place in a bowl together with above fruit and mixed peel. Sift the flour into a clean bowl and work in the minced beef suet. Rub well into flour then add sugar and salt. Mix thoroughly. Break the eggs into a bowl and beat until smooth. Add to suet. Add fruit, peel, grated nutmeg, almonds and walnuts to the suet and mix well. Add the brandy and rum. The mixture should be quite moist. Refrigerate for 24 hours then place the pudding mixture into a clean cloth or buttered bowl. Place in boiling water and boil for 5 hours, reduce heat, cover with a lid and continue to steam for a further 3 hours. Remove from water and cool completely. Place the pudding in a double layer of muslin and allow it to hang for 2-6 weeks before use. Every 3 days pour a little additional brandy and rum over the pudding to keep moist. If preferred, the fruit may be soaked in brandy for several weeks beforehand. Serve hot with brandy sauce or butter.

BRANDY SAUCE

1 teaspoon cornflour
150 ml milk
1 teaspoon sugar
1 egg yolk
200 ml brandy

Blend the cornflour with a little of the milk and reserve. Heat the remaining milk and bring to the boil. Remove from heat and add the cornflour, stirring continuously to prevent lumps. When smooth, return to a low heat and add the sugar. When sugar has dissolved, remove from heat and allow to cool slightly. Beat the egg yolk until smooth. Add, stirring, to the sauce. Return to the heat and continue to cook, adding the brandy a little at a time. When sauce thickens, remove from heat and serve immediately.

BRANDY BUTTER

200 g butter
75 g icing sugar
brandy

Place the butter in a bowl and sift in the icing sugar. Beat with a wooden spoon until smooth and creamy. Add brandy to taste. Refrigerate for a few minutes before use.

CANDIED BANANAS

6 green bananas
50 g butter
25 g sugar
2 teaspoons cinnamon
300 ml orange juice
100 g orange marmalade
50 g chopped almonds
50 g cornflour

serves 6

Wash and wipe the bananas and cut in halves lengthwise (do not remove skins). Melt the butter in a frying pan, add sugar and cinnamon. Gently sauté the banana halves for 2 minutes, remove from pan, drain and place on a warm serving dish in a low oven. Add orange juice to the pan and bring to the boil. Add orange marmalade and stir until smooth. Add the chopped almonds and reduce heat to simmer. Blend the cornflour with a little cold water and stir into the orange sauce. When thickened slightly, pour sauce over the bananas and serve immediately with vanilla ice cream.

CHERRIES JUBILEE

450 g cherries
275 ml water
100 g sugar
170 g redcurrant jelly
2 drops orange essence
1 teaspoon icing sugar
50 ml kirsch

serves 4

Wash the cherries, pat dry and remove stalks and stones. Place in a saucepan with water and sugar. Cover and cook for 10 minutes. Stir in the redcurrant jelly, orange essence and icing sugar and cook for a further 3 minutes. Strain and place cherries in a serving dish. Return juice to saucepan and reduce liquid by two-thirds. Cover the cherries with the syrup and keep dish warm on the side of the stove or in the oven. Warm the kirsch in a clean saucepan and when ready for serving, place the dish on the table, pour over the warmed kirsch and set alight to flame.

ZABAGLIONE

225 g castor sugar
6 egg yolks
150 ml dry white wine
150 ml marsala or port

serves 6

Beat the sugar and egg yolks together then transfer to a double saucepan. When the water in lower half of saucepan is boiling rapidly, place the top in position and beat the egg mixture continuously until it is light and frothy. It must be thick enough to form peaks. Slowly add the wine and continue to beat for a further 10 minutes. Add the marsala, a little at a time and continue to beat the mixture until thick. Pour into parfait glasses and serve immediately.
NOTE: Champagne can be used in place of white wine.

WATERMELON FRUIT SALAD

½ **watermelon**
½ **pineapple**
1 **apple**
4 **passionfruit**
50 ml **pineapple juice**
50 ml **orange juice**
100 ml **kirsch**
275 ml **whipped cream**
lemon juice

serves 4

Using a melon baller, scoop out the flesh of watermelon, removing seeds and place in a glass salad bowl. Reserve a few melon balls for decoration. Cut rind from pineapple, core and cut into bite-sized pieces. Halve some of the rings and place along the sides of the salad bowl. Peel, core and slice the apple. Sprinkle with lemon juice to prevent browning and add to fruit salad. Combine the pineapple and orange juice with the kirsch and pour over the fruit. Top with reserved melon balls and passionfruit and serve well chilled with whipped cream. If desired, castor sugar may be sprinkled on top.

STRAWBERRIES IN ORANGE JUICE

2 punnets strawberries
275 ml whipped cream

SAUCE
275 ml fresh orange juice
75 ml curaçao
50 g icing sugar

serves 4

Wash the strawberries and remove stalks. Drain and reserve. Dissolve the icing sugar in a little boiled orange juice. Stir in the remaining orange juice and curaçao. Place the sauce in refrigerator until quite chilled. Cut the strawberries in half and place around the sides of individual dessert glasses, facing upwards. Fill the centre of the glasses with whole fruit. Pour the sauce over the top to approximately 25 mm from bottom of glass. Whip the cream until fairly stiff. Either place on top of strawberries or serve separately.

Strawberries in Orange Juice

FLAKY PASTRY

100 g lard
225 g butter
450 g plain flour
1 teaspoon salt
175 ml cold water
25 ml lemon juice

Blend together the lard and butter and form it into a square. Divide into 4 equal portions and refrigerate for 30 minutes to set. Sift the flour and salt together into a mixing bowl. Divide one portion of the shortening into small lumps and rub into the flour with the fingertips until the mixture resembles fine breadcrumbs. Make a well in the centre and pour in 250 ml cold water. Using a spatula or flat knife stir vigorously, adding lemon juice a little at a time and working continually until the dough is smooth and comes away from the sides of the bowl without sticking. If mixture is too dry, slowly add a teaspoon of water at a time, until the dough is of the right consistency. Knead with the hands for a few minutes then cover dough with a clean cloth and leave to stand in a cool place for 30 minutes. Turn on to a floured board and roll out into a rectangle. Dab small pieces of the second portion of shortening evenly over the top two-thirds of the pastry leaving a 25 mm border all around. Fold the bottom third of the pastry upwards and the top third downwards to cover it. Seal the edges with the handle of a knife. Give the pastry a half turn (so the fold is on your left) and roll pastry by pressing twice with rolling pin so as to trap as much air as possible. Roll out into a rectangle and add the third portion of shortening and roll up as before. Repeat the rolling once more using the last portion of shortening, roll out, fold and seal for the fourth time (without shortening). Cover and leave to stand for 30 minutes in a cool place before use.

RUFF PUFF PASTRY

225 g plain flour
pinch salt
170 g butter
1 egg yolk
few drops lemon juice
iced water

Sift the flour and salt into a bowl and mix to rolling consistency with cold water and lemon juice. Add the beaten egg yolk and work mixture for a few minutes then set aside for 15 minutes. Take the butter and place it in the middle of the dough. Fold the bottom section of the pastry over the butter first and then the top section so that the butter is completely covered. Turn the dough at right angles, seal edges and roll out. Fold dough into an envelope, turn it, seal edges and roll again. Repeat this process 5 times, chilling the pastry in the refrigerator for 15 minutes in between each rolling (wrap in greaseproof paper). Finally, unwrap pastry and roll once more. Use immediately or store in refrigerator in a damp cloth until ready for use.

SHORTCRUST PASTRY

225 g plain flour
25 g vegetable fat
25 g lard
25 g butter
½ teaspoon salt
50-75 g cold water

Sift the flour and salt into a mixing bowl. Mix the 3 shortenings together then work them into the flour, using the fingertips and raising the flour as high as possible to allow air into the mixture. When mixture resembles fine breadcrumbs, stir in the water and mix thoroughly with a fork. When smooth, work the dough with your hands for a few minutes. The consistency should be such that the bowl is left clean when dough is rubbed around the sides. Add more water or sifted flour to adjust the consistency. Turn the dough out onto a floured board and knead for a few minutes then roll out to desired shape. To store in refrigerator, wrap the pastry in greaseproof paper then in a damp cloth.

SWEET SHORTCRUST PASTRY

225 g plain flour
50 g icing sugar
½ teaspoon salt
150 g margarine
cold milk

Sift the flour, icing sugar and salt into a bowl. Cut the margarine into small lumps and drop them into the flour, coating each one well. Using the fingertips, rub the shortening into the flour using the same method as for shortcrust pastry (above). When mixture resembles fine breadcrumbs, mix in the milk, using a fork, until the dough is pliable and non-sticky. Work the dough with the palms of your hands for a few minutes before turning out onto a floured board. Knead lightly then roll out to desired shape or store in the refrigerator until ready for use.

NOTE: For savoury pastry, use the shortcrust basic recipe and add parsley, chives, mixed herbs, garlic salt, marjoram or other herbs. For additional flavour to sweet shortcrust pastry, use the basic recipe above and add cinnamon, nutmeg, allspice, vanilla, almond essence etc.

BÉCHAMEL SAUCE

840 ml milk
1 stalk celery
1 carrot
1 parsnip
1 turnip
1 pinch thyme
1 bay leaf
1 sprig parsley
75 g butter
75 g flour
salt and pepper
grated nutmeg

Place the milk in a large saucepan or in the top of a double boiler. Wash and trim the celery and carrot and slice. Peel the parsnip and turnip and dice roughly. Add vegetables to milk and slowly bring to the boil, reduce to simmer and cook for 15 minutes. Add thyme, bay leaf and parsley and cook for a further 20 minutes over a very slow heat. Strain the milk through a muslin cloth and discard vegetables and herbs. Melt the butter in a deep pan and stir in the flour to make a white (blonde) roux. Cook for 1 minute then remove from heat and slowly pour in a little of the milk, stirring until smooth. Gradually add the rest of the milk, whisking to prevent lumps. Add salt and pepper to taste. Return sauce to heat — do not boil. When sauce has become thick and creamy, remove from heat and serve immediately.

BUTTER SAUCE

25 g flour
25 g butter
225 g additional butter
100 ml white vinegar
salt
white pepper

Make a roux by blending the flour and butter in a saucepan. Cook for 1 minute then reduce heat. Add the additional butter, a little at a time, stirring to prevent lumps. When all the butter has been used, whisk the mixture until it becomes creamy but do not allow to boil. Continue to whisk whilst adding the vinegar, a little at a time. When the mixture has thickened slightly and is creamy in texture, add salt and white pepper to taste. Serve immediately with fish, asparagus, artichokes or broccoli.

BUTTER HERB SAUCE

25 g flour
25 g butter
225 g additional butter
3 shallots
50 ml dry white wine
25 g parsley
1 teaspoon basil
1 teaspoon sage
salt
pepper

Melt the butter in a frying pan and stir in the flour. When smooth, remove from heat and add additional butter, mixing thoroughly. Return to heat and stir for a few minutes or until mixture is creamy. Transfer to a saucepan and place over a low heat and whisk until thickened slightly. Peel and finely dice the shallots. Add to sauce. Slowly pour in the dry white wine and continue to whisk for 3 minutes. Add the parsley, basil, sage, salt and pepper to taste. Serve with fish, shellfish or green vegetables.

MADEIRA SAUCE

75 g belly pork
50 g streaky bacon
1 carrot
2 onions
1 stalk celery
1 parsnip
1 bay leaf
1 bouquet garni
200 ml rich stock
100 ml dry white wine
250 ml madeira
50 g butter
75 g flour
salt
black pepper

Place the belly pork and bacon in a heavy-based pan and cook over a high heat for 15 minutes to extract all the fat. Remove meat and discard. Finely slice the carrot, peel and dice the onions, cut celery in half, peel and dice the parsnip. Place the vegetables, 1 type at a time, in the pork and bacon fat and sauté until golden brown. Drain vegetables and transfer to a large saucepan. Add bay leaf, bouquet garni and stock. Bring to the boil and cook for 15 minutes then reduce heat and simmer for a further 15 minutes. Add the dry white wine and madeira and continue to cook over a low heat for a further 15 minutes. Strain stock and set aside. Squeeze vegetables and herbs against the side of a sieve to extract all their juices then discard the pulp. In a clean frying pan make a roux by melting the butter and stirring in the flour, cook for 3 minutes then remove from heat and gradually stir in the stock, a little at a time, until mixture is smooth. Return to heat and cook for a few minutes without boiling. Serve with offal, ham, cooked meats or vegetables.

MAYONNAISE

2 egg yolks, at room temperature
250 ml olive oil
25 ml lemon juice
25 ml tarragon vinegar
1 teaspoon chilli powder
1 teaspoon mustard powder
1 pinch sugar
salt
white pepper

Place the 'room temperature' egg yolks in a bowl and beat with a wooden spoon until smooth. Add olive oil in a thin stream, whisking continuously with a wire whisk until mixture becomes thick and creamy. Add lemon juice and continue to beat. When quite firm, mix the vinegar, chilli powder, mustard and sugar together and add to the mayonnaise and continue to beat until smooth. Serve immediately, or if mayonnaise is to be stored in the refrigerator for the following day, stir 25 ml of boiling water into the thickened mixture. This will prevent it from separating.

Variations: Add finely chopped parsley, chives, chervil and tarragon for fish or shellfish.
Season with 25 g curry powder and 1 teaspoon turmeric for cold chicken or fish.
Beat in 100 ml cream and a dash of nutmeg for vegetables, especially asparagus.
Beat in 100 ml cream, 1 teaspoon tabasco, 1 teaspoon worcestershire sauce and 25 ml tomato sauce for seafood cocktails.

MUSTARD SAUCE

2 egg yolks
1 teaspoon sugar
25 g mustard powder
2 teaspoons wine vinegar
200 ml olive oil
1 pinch tarragon
1 pinch salt
freshly ground white pepper
25 ml lemon juice

Place the egg yolks in a bowl with sugar and mustard and whisk until smooth and creamy. Pour the wine vinegar and olive oil into the eggs in alternate streams, a little at a time and whisking all the time. When the mixture is thick and creamy, beat in the tarragon, salt, pepper and lemon juice. Serve with fish. This sauce is especially good with pickled fish.

SAUCE ESPAGNOLE

75 g lard or dripping
4 rashers streaky bacon
1 onion
1 stalk celery
1 carrot
1 turnip
1 potato
75 g cornflour or arrowroot
2 litres beef stock
1 bouquet garni
1 clove garlic
1 bay leaf
150 ml tomato purée
salt and pepper

Melt the fat in a heavy-based frying pan and add the chopped rashers of bacon. Peel and dice the onion, slice celery and carrot, peel and finely dice the turnip and potato. Add vegetables to the fat and bacon and fry until golden brown. Mix the cornflour with a little of the stock. Set aside. Pour remaining stock into a large saucepan and add the drained vegetables and bacon, bouquet garni, sliced garlic and bay leaf. Bring to the boil then reduce heat and simmer gently with the lid on, for 1½ hours. Skim the top from time to time to remove any excess fat or scum. Strain the stock through a fine sieve or muslin cloth and place in a clean saucepan. Bring to the boil and reduce liquid by two-thirds, lower heat and stir in the tomato purée. When smooth, add the reserved cornflour and stir until the mixture thickens. Season to taste with salt and pepper and serve immediately or store in a screw-top jar in the refrigerator until ready for use. Serve with meat dishes and pasta. This makes a good basic sauce for spaghetti with meat sauce.

SAUCE VERTE

275 ml mayonnaise
50 g parsley
25 g chervil
25 g watercress, minced
25 g spinach leaves, minced
1 teaspoon sweet marjoram
25 ml lemon juice
salt and pepper

Place mayonnaise, parsley, chervil, minced watercress, minced spinach leaves, and sweet marjoram in an electric blender. When smooth and creamy, transfer to a bowl and mix in the lemon juice, salt and pepper to taste. Serve with fish dishes. If desired 1 teaspoon of tarragon or dillweed can be added.

TARTARE SAUCE

4 hard-boiled eggs
salt
black pepper
275 ml olive oil
25 ml wine vinegar
75 g mayonnaise
25 g chopped chives
25 g capers

Remove the yolks from hard-boiled eggs and push through a fine sieve then place in a bowl and mash with salt and black pepper. Using a fork, gradually whisk in the oil and vinegar in alternate streams. Add the mayonnaise and stir until smooth. Chop the chives and capers then pound them in a mortar. When pounded into a paste, stir into the sauce and serve immediately with fish.
NOTE: A teaspoon of lemon juice can be added if desired

TOMATO SAUCE

12 large ripe tomatoes
2 onions
1 stalk celery
1 carrot
4 cloves garlic
1 bouquet garni
1 bay leaf
12 cloves
25 g cayenne pepper
2 teaspoons mixed herbs
1 teaspoon allspice
150 ml dry white wine
100 ml malt vinegar
435 ml vegetable stock
salt
pepper
sugar

Place tomatoes in a large bowl and pour boiling water over to crack skins. Remove skins and cores and cut tomatoes into quarters. Peel and slice the onions finely, slice celery, carrot and garlic. Place vegetables in a saucepan with remaining ingredients and bring to the boil. Cook for 15 minutes then reduce heat, cover and simmer for 1 hour. Strain the vegetables and place in an electric blender set at stir/mix or push through a mouli, leaving seeds of tomatoes intact. Reserve the purée. Return stock to saucepan and simmer over a gentle heat for 3 hours. Increase heat to high for 30 minutes then remove from stove and stir in the purée. Season to taste with salt, pepper and sugar. Use with pasta, meat, eggs, vegetables or fish.

VELOUTÉ SAUCE

75 g butter
75 g flour
650 ml veal stock
75 g cultivated mushrooms
salt
pepper

Melt the butter in a saucepan, stir in the sifted flour and cook for 1 minute. Remove from heat and slowly pour in the veal stock, stirring to prevent lumps. Return to heat and stir until thickened. Wipe and trim the mushrooms, chop roughly and add both mushrooms and trimmings to the sauce. Cook very slowly until the volume is reduced by half. When the sauce is thick and creamy, strain through a muslin cloth, season to taste, re-heat and serve immediately.

Glossary

Bake Method of cooking pies, pastries, biscuits etc. in the oven. Term also applied to roasting meat and vegetables, mainly used in America.

Bake blind To bake pastry cases without a filling. The bottom of the pastry is lined with greaseproof paper and sprinkled with raw rice grains, bread crusts or lentils. These items absorb most of the heat which prevents drying out and burning.

Barquettes Small pastry cases (sweet or savoury) baked in a boat-shaped mould.

Beurre Manié Equal portions of butter and flour gently kneaded together to form a smooth mixture and placed in small amounts into liquid as a thickening agent.

Bind Method of making a dry mixture adhere with the use of egg yolks.

Blanch To whiten chicken, sweetbreads, tripe, veal etc by placing in cold water and bringing to the boil. Also the method used for removing skins from tomatoes, fruit and nuts by plunging into boiling water, and for the removal of excess salt from vegetables.

Clarify Butter: Place butter in a saucepan and bring to the boil taking care that it does not burn. When a white scum appears on top, remove from heat and set aside for the sediment to settle. Strain through a double layer of muslin cloth and discard residue.
Stock or Broth: Place liquid in a saucepan and for every 1½ litres use 2 egg whites and their washed, crushed shells. Whisk briskly whilst bringing to the boil. Beat for 5 minutes then strain liquid through a double layer of muslin. For a clearer liquid, repeat the above process using 1 egg white and 1 crushed shell.

Curry powder The following are basic ingredients and can be adjusted according to individual palates.
Fish: 50 g coriander seeds, 25 g fennel seeds, 50 g dried chillies, 25 g garam masala, 25 g black peppercorns, 1 teaspoon turmeric powder, 2 teaspoons cumin seeds.
Poultry: 6-8 dried chillies, 50 g coriander seeds, 50 g mustard seeds, 25 g peppercorns, 25 g cumin seeds, 25 mm turmeric root, 25 mm ginger root, 4 cloves garlic.
Meat: 50 g coriander seeds, 50 g cumin seeds, 50 g turmeric, 25 g cayenne pepper, 50 mm cinnamon stick, 25 ml lemon juice, 5 dried red chillies, 5 cardamom pods, 3 cloves, 1 teaspoon fenugreek, 1 teaspoon ginger.
To prepare the curry powder, remove seeds from pods, wash whole spices and dry in the sun. When dry place in the oven and cook for 30 minutes. Place all dry ingredients into an electric blender or coffee grinder and mix to a fine powder.

Devil	To fry over rapid heat in butter and salt (especially for almonds) or to grill food with butter, mustard, worcestershire sauce and fresh breadcrumbs.
Dice	To cut into small, even-sized cubes.
Dry fry	Frying of food, usually minced meat, without fat or any other shortening. This method removes excess fat from meat and results in fast browning.
Flame	Also flamber which is the French word for setting alight, usually by pouring warmed cognac or other alcohol over food and setting alight to burn out excess butter and to seal in delicate flavours.
Julienne	Meat or vegetables cut into match-like strips. The easiest way to achieve this is by use of a mandolin.
Knead	Working dough with the palms of the hands, pulling each side to the centre then patting the dough rigorously before rolling out.
Marinade	A highly flavoured liquid which can be cooked or uncooked, consisting of red or white wine, sherry, oil, vinegar, herbs, spices, honey, soya sauce and/or vegetables in which meat and fish are left for lengthy periods of time to soak up the delicate flavours. It is also a means of tenderising meat and breaking down fat cells.
Reduce	Rapid boiling down, uncovered, of liquid. Usually used for nondescript-tasting stocks, which, when reduced, become tasty concentrated fluids which are used for sauces, gravies and casseroles.
Roast	Cooking meat or vegetables in an oven. Often referred to as baking.
Roux	Pale: Also Blonde, White. Melted butter in which flour is gently blended over a low heat and cooked for 1 minute before removing from heat and adding liquid. It must not take on colour. Brown: Same method as for pale but is cooked for 2-3 minutes or until the colour becomes a soft golden brown and imparts a delicate nutty aroma. Brown roux can also be cooked in a baking dish in the oven. A roux is used for thickening casseroles, stews, soups, etc., and is capable of absorbing 5-6 times it's own weight when cooked.
Santan	First and second santans are used in curry making. They are used basically to tenderise meat, and give the distinctive flavour to some of the Indian and Malaysian curries. If fresh coconut is not available, soak 250 g dessicated coconut in 500 ml boiling water. Squeeze thoroughly and reserve the 'milk' which is the second santan. Repeat the process using the same coconut for the first santan. The stronger or second santan plays the more important role in curry making.

Sauté Gentle frying of vegetables, meat or fish in very little fat or butter and to more rapid frying of meats which are quickly browned on all sides by shaking the pan frequently to prevent burning. Also referred to as sealing.

Seal Refer to 'Sauté'.

Steep To set aside and allow food to absorb the flavour of marinades, herbs, spices and condiments.

Stir-fry A Chinese method of rapid cooking, usually in a wok where vegetables and sometimes meat, are fried in very little oil over a fierce heat. The result is that vegetables retain their vital crispiness and meat juices are completely sealed in. Cooking time is anywhere between ½-2 minutes depending on the ingredient being cooked. This must not be confused with the European method of frying which normally renders vegetables soggy.

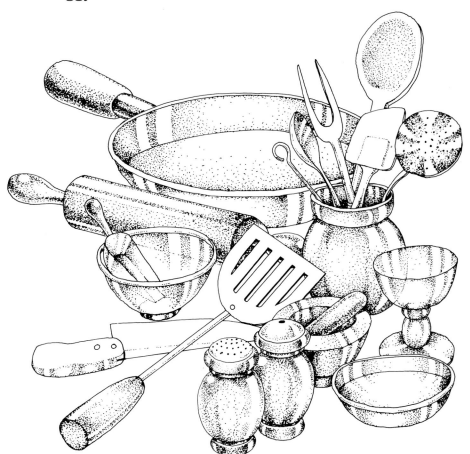

List of Colour Plates

Food prepared and cooked by Helen Fleming
Photography by Benno Gross Associates

Index

MAIN COURSES